The Crystal Stair

Grace Chetwin

THE CRYSTAL STAIR

FROM
Tales of Gom
IN THE
LEGENDS OF ULM

Bradbury Press · *New York*

Special Acknowledgments

to Joseph & Susan Iadone:
to Joe, for his wonderful guitar settings to the songs,
and to Susan for playing the lyrics on the viol to his
accompaniment, so that we could hear them at their best.

Bradbury Press
An Affiliate of Macmillan, Inc.
866 Third Avenue, New York, N.Y. 10022
Collier Macmillan Canada, Inc.
Printed and bound in the United States of America
10 9 8 7 6 5 4 3 2 1

The text of this book is set in 12 pt. Garamond #3.

The map of Ulm is based on the one Carrick the tinker gave Gom.

Library of Congress Cataloging-in-Publication Data

Chetwin, Grace.
The crystal stair : from tales of Gom in the legends of Ulm / Grace
Chetwin.
p.   cm.
Sequel to: The riddle & the rune.
Summary: Temporarily reunited with his wizard mother, Gom learns
the identity of his evil nemesis Katak and finds himself a key figure in
the battle to save the world of Ulm from destruction.
ISBN 0-02-718311-4
{1. Fantasy.}   I. Title. PZ7.C42555Cr 1988 {Fic}—dc19
87-27395 CIP AC

For Dorothy Crossley
Teacher and friend
With love

GREAT

RINGING
VALLEY

THE WILDS

DUNDERFOSSE

SUNDOR
Sundborg

SOUTHERN

KRUGK

HIGH VARGUE

Quend

Green Vale

Bragget-on-the-Edge

LONG VALLEY

Lake Langoth

Pen'langoth

SHORE

Chapter One

THEY CLIMBED the narrow winding path single file: Harga first, then Gom, striking his staff into the ground to propel himself up. Stormfleet followed, the irregular clop of the colt's hooves muffled by thick deadfall on the forest floor. Mossy trunks, like pillars of some primeval fortress, tilted toward a canopy of distant branches that swayed and creaked like old bones.

Gom heaved a satisfied sigh: all those years of wishing for his mother, and here she was.

Harga paused, looking back, patiently waiting for him and Stormfleet to catch up. She was, he noticed as he reached her, not even out of breath.

Gom was tired already, though it was but midmorning. Not so much from the climb, he being a mountain boy, as from excitement at their meeting, and the hour's walk to reach this slope. "How much farther?"

"Almost there." Harga's smile gave way to mild concern. "You look pale. How's the head?" She reached out, lifted his tangled hair to inspect the swollen gash on his temple from his fall in the solahinn stockade.

"I'm fine," he said, squirming. "Ready for elevenses!"

"Elevenses?" At the word, a favorite of Stig's, Harga's eyes flickered. For a moment, Gom thought he saw hurt, or even anger, but then her long, solemn face cleared. "Oh, dear, you've not had breakfast yet, and it's nearly noon! Some mother I'm proving to be!" She looked past Gom to Stormfleet, bared her teeth, blew her lips out with force, and addressed the cito colt in his own tongue. "We have to go a little farther up the tail end of this mountain spur. I hope you don't find the ground too troublesome."

Stormfleet shook his mane. "Thank you, when I do I'll let you know it!"

Harga, laughing, patted his side. "You do that, my young friend," she said, and moved on.

Gom listened with great satisfaction to his mother conversing with Stormfleet in the cito's own speech. He'd always thought that it was from her that his own gift had come. No other humans in the world besides them could speak the tongues of beasts, so Stormfleet said. Behind him, the cito slipped, *frrrupped* in irritation. Born of the plains, he didn't take as kindly to climbing as he'd have Harga think, Gom was sure.

A map lay folded in Gom's jacket pocket. With that map, Harga had shown that they were in the Dunderfosse: magical forest; vast, primal tract between the Wilds to the east, and a mass of snowpeaks down its western side. From these peaks, the spur they climbed tapered like a tail down into the treetops.

Gom breathed deep, expelled the air with pleasure, feeling more and more at home among the gloomy trunks and rising slopes.

The ground got steeper, yet still the forest persisted as though reluctant to give ground within its fastnesses.

But at last, undergrowth dwindled to open spaces; deadfall, to a mat of dry brown needles. Boulders lay about like huddled sheep.

All at once, Gom caught the tang of resin.

Pines.

He slowed and looked around, thinking of Windy Mountain, and the log cabin Stig his father had built, then enlarged for his and Harga's growing family. Ten children, of whom Gom was the last. He sighed, staring through the dimness, remembering.

Before leaving home to find his mother, Gom had buried Stig by the front door, and raised a tall cairn over his venerable head. Owl had uttered eulogy, and Wind had keened among the frozen stones. And his mother's rune, briefly sparking to life, had made strange sweet music to mourn the passing.

"Gom." Harga turned him about, and pressed him to her silently.

Her embrace felt stiff and awkward; her small, slight body, unfamiliar. Only two other women had ever held him thus: Hilsa, his sister, and Mudge, the motherly farmer's wife near Green Vale who'd nursed him back to health. Big, matronly women they were, generous bodies engulfing him in warmth.

But this was his mother! Impulsively, he returned her squeeze, catching, as he had at their joyous meeting, the faint dry smell of her skin, and a whiff of wintergreen from the folds of her shawl.

Stormfleet trod somewhere near, cracking brittle needles under his hooves. Stig's walking stick—Gom's staff— which Gom had slipped under his arm in order to hug

Harga—was now poking his ribs painfully. He shifted, trying to ease his growing discomfort without breaking that moment, but Harga pulled back, took a large brown handkerchief from her brown skirt pocket, and blew her nose with vigor.

"What a day." She stuffed the handkerchief back in her pocket. "Come on. Let's get you home. We have so much to talk about. And you look more in need of— elevenses—by the minute." She spun around, hitched her skirt above her high brown boots, and strode off again.

Gom started after her, thinking. While Stig had grieved for Harga until his dying day, it was becoming clear that Harga had missed Stig no less.

Stig had never ceased to talk of her, and to remark proudly how Gom took after her in every way, not least in looks. "Like you, son," his father would declare. "You're her very double."

Gom's lips parted suddenly.

That this woman, with the long face, long, bent nose, sharp eyes, and long brown hair coiled at her nape, was his mother, Gom had no doubt. But—he recalled Stig sitting by the fire, his fair hair turned white, his limbs enfeebled with age—after all those years, she was still as Stig remembered her: *aged not one whit!* He eyed the small figure climbing sturdily before him. Was she not the greatest wizard in all Ulm? That surely would have something to do with it. Nodding, he moved on.

The ground grew steeper. Stormfleet struck his hoof against rock, shied skittishly. Gom stopped, waited for his friend to recover.

"I'm fine," Stormfleet snapped. "Let's keep going."

Almost home, Harga had said. What was a little more discomfort now? He was with his mother at last, with all the time in the world to learn of her wizardry, and fit himself for the danger ahead. And ahead it surely was. For though Harga hadn't said, the thought of Katak lay between them.

He firmly pushed that grim thought aside to think on Harga's house. Was it like their old cabin? If not, he could make it more so, add touches of Stig, carve bits and pieces after his father's way. Wouldn't she be glad to have him then!

Of course, she'd expected him. Had already mentioned that he had his own room. Had she some magic ready for them to make together? His first lesson? Gom tried to imagine Harga's workshop, what he'd find there. Jewels, he was sure, for hadn't Ganash told him that "from precious gold and silver and priceless gemstones is much magic made." Making magic, he decided, must be somewhat like cooking: a bit of this, a pinch of that, mixing them up, setting them to brew. In that case, she'd have bowls and spoons, and dishes. And bottles to store things in. Stig had spoken many times about the glass jars in which Harga kept the makings of remedies for the family. Those she'd taken with her when she left. A wave of impatience spurred him up the slope to the crest where Harga already stood, gazing down the other side.

"Here we are."

Gom looked out expectantly. The spur curved away to distant peaks that reared above the treetops. But directly before them was a green-clad dip, round and smooth as a pudding basin. In the middle of the basin was a lake.

In the middle of the lake was an island, a plug of sandstone cliff high as the tall, three-storied houses Gom had seen in Pen'langoth.

He scrutinized the cliff's flat bare top, the sweep of wooded shore, but saw no sign of dwelling. "Where?"

Harga pointed to the island. "There. Come on." She started down to the water's edge.

As Gom hesitated, eyeing the waves from cliff to shore, Stormfleet pawed the ground uneasily. Gom stroked his neck in sympathy. "I hate water, you hate heights, and here we are, headed for a mountain lake. Courage."

"It's all very well for you to say." Stormfleet started down, grumbling.

Harga was already waiting on the shore—or, rather, off the shore, on a small log raft that bobbed in the waves. She beckoned them to join her. "The raft will feel unsafe at first, my young friend," she warned the cito, "but in fact it could carry a dozen folk with no trouble."

Nevertheless, Stormfleet watched Gom get on first. Only then did the colt step nervously across. The raft dipped, and bobbed, awash with waves, and Stormfleet shied, but Harga and Gom caught him, held him steady until the bouncing stopped. Harga took up a long paddle and pushed off from the shore.

"Here, Mother. Let me." Gom set down his staff, and reached to help.

Harga shook her head. "I'm used to it, thank you."

Gom stood stiffly looking out, dashed at her refusal. But as they neared the cliff, he was glad Harga had taken on the paddling, for it gave him chance to take a good first view of his new home—Harga's aim all along, he'd bet. He relaxed, drawing in the high, clear air, while

Harga paddled and poled away. By the time they moved under the lee of the island cliff, he was cheery again.

The yellow sandstone face, Gom saw, was pocked with holes, the sort that swallows nested in. Sure enough, just then a brown bank swallow swooped out from one, caught an amber damselfly, and started back again.

Harga followed the island around to the western side, where Gom got a surprise. The cliff was not the solid plug it seemed, but hollow, like a crescent moon, bounded by a strip of sandy shore. Behind the shore curved a hedge of dark green holly. Was Harga's house behind that?

Gom helped beach the raft, then eagerly pushed his way through the prickly screen to the other side, where he pulled up in surprise. Every inch of the level space from hedge to cliff was garden: neat beds of vegetables and herbs, clumps of flowering shrubs, orchard—and beehives! The green of vegetables was splashed by bright flowers: lavender and lilies, stocks, and daisies, and snapdragons, portulaca, poppies and anemones, regardless of their proper season. Birds flew everywhere, and clouds of insects hummed through the heady air.

Gom gazed about, minded of his brother Stok's vegetable patch, and his sister Hilsa's flower beds, and her hives, and recognized now Harga's influence. A wonderful garden indeed—but *where was the house!*

He finally lit upon a low shed at the far side, with plain thatched roof, a narrow dark doorway—no door, and but a hole for window. A fat nanny goat sauntered out, bleated a lazy good morning, then put her head down to graze.

Gom looked at the shed in dismay. That was it?

"Good morning, Jillifer!" Harga called to the nanny

goat. "Jilly's been with me since she was a newborn kid, as her mother before her," she told Gom, then added with a wave to the shed behind Jilly. "That's my barn-cum-dairy."

"Oh." Gom relaxed. "And the house?"

Harga jabbed a finger triumphantly at the curving cliff. "Why, there."

Gom stared.

"You still can't see, can you?" She laughed out loud. "Good. Wizards don't like their houses to show, even under your very nose. See those holes? The small ones harbor swallows' nests. The larger ones? My windows! Come, see. But first"—she turned to Stormfleet—"let's make you welcome, friend."

She led the colt to the orchard, to a patch of grazing watered by a quick spring. "You'll be comfortable for a while?"

Stormfleet sampled the grass, then whuffled with pleasure. "Take your time. Don't mind me. This is good!"

Harga led Gom along a pebble path to a spot midway along the cliff base, and pressed a crack waist-high in the stone. A narrow slab swung inward, a cunning door cut into massive sandstone wall.

Harga stepped through, Gom after. The slab closed with a *thock,* shutting out the lap of water, and the noise of bird and insect, leaving them in sudden cool and quiet. At last Gom understood, and marveled. The crescent cliff was hollow.

They stood in a low cave spanning the width of the cliff from east to west. The morning sunlight beamed in through clustered holes in the opposite, eastern wall, reflecting off blue-washed stone the color of the summer sky. Gom crossed over, and looking out, saw waves dancing just below his feet.

"My front hall," Harga said. "The rest of the house is upstairs."

A narrow spiral stair cut into the far wall brought Gom up into a second-story passage that curved the length of the cliff on either hand. The passage was blue-washed, like the rest of the house, and flooded with light from doorways in both east and western walls.

Harga took the one directly opposite the stairwell.

Gom followed.

Two paces in, he stopped, looking in astonishment on Harga's kitchen, hung with pots and pans, lined with shelves for dishes and utensils and jars of herbs and spices. A cave, transformed into Stig's cabin: log walls and beams, stone hearth and two small windows—even loft and ladder!

Gom climbed the ladder, and peered into the loft above, half expecting to find old sleeping pallets, relics of Stig's crowded family. But the bare scrubbed boards smelled of root and apple: Harga's winter storage place under curving sandstone roof.

"You like it?" Harga called. "Come, see your room."

She drew him back out into the hall, then led him right. Past the open doors, Gom glimpsed small chambers; more caves, all with scattered round windows letting in light, brilliant sunshine on the eastern side. So this was his mother's house—a stranger place than he could ever imagine: a wizard's house, and his, too, now. He thought of the years to come in this wonderful house—he and Harga, two wizards working their magic peacefully together— His face clouded. He was forgetting Katak. Could he speak of that now? He shot Harga a look. No. This was not yet the time.

Gom's bedchamber was four doors down from the kitchen, on the same side, facing east into the morning sun. It was low and small, a comfortable space that put him in mind of the little lean-to in Hort and Mudge's house. A bright red mat ran from the door to the most remarkable bed Gom had ever seen. Its carved headboard stood the height of the right-hand wall, not overly high, but massive enough in that small room. A carved wooden hoot owl presided over the top rail in the angle between wall and curved ceiling, its small, stern eye fixed on Gom. Not as good as Stig's handiwork, lacking the fine, sure detail that made Stig's animals spring from the wood seemingly alive, but well enough. The counterpane was a crocheted blanket worked with suns and moons and stars, like the one Harga had given Stig.

Gom set down pack and staff, and tested the bed. It was soft and bouncy, with, he lifted the cover, smooth white sheets that smelled of lavender.

Across the bed, in the outer wall, was a large oval window. Gom slid across the counterpane, and, leaning into the deep sill, gazed into the high morning sun, to the ridge they'd climbed.

A swallow shot past, making Gom jump, and alighted twittering shrilly in its hole somewhere above, telling, if Gom heard aright, of the human fledgling that had just flown into its mother's nest, and the strangeness of human ways. Smiling, he turned back into the room, to find his mother still standing in the doorway, watching.

He felt a sudden awkwardness. "You never wanted to leave us, did you?"

Harga shook her head. "No." She advanced into the room, her face sad. She'd not had an easy time of it on Windy Mountain, Gom knew. And after she left, folk had condemned her for, as they were pleased to say, heartlessly abandoning her brood. Unfair! It had been hard enough to take his leave of Stok and Hilsa, and even Hort and Mudge. How much harder it must have been for Harga to leave her family of thirteen long years.

Gom pictured her returning to this lonely place, re-shaping her kitchen cave into that cabin, thinking of Stig. She must have felt such a loss to have done that. At least, he thought, he and Stig had had each other. He seized up his staff and held it out.

"Father made this just before he died. Take it."

Harga closed her hand upon it, ran her thin brown fingers over the carved animals leaping and twisting about the stave: snake, and rabbit, and turtle and mouse, and pert brown sparrow perched on top. "Keep it," she said. "It will make a fine wizard's staff one day."

Wizard's staff.

Gom's hand went to his chest, but of course, the stone wasn't there. He'd returned his mother's magic rune hours since, and it was hanging at her chest now. Would he ever grow used to its loss?

Harga drew him to the door. "Come on, if you're a true sprig off the bush, you're starving. Your father always ate enough for six!"

As they turned to go back to the kitchen, Gom caught

sight of another stair at the end of the passage, going up again. "Where does that lead?"

"To my workshop," she said.

Harga's workshop! Gom's heart did a little jig. "May I see?"

Harga smiled faintly. "Perhaps after you've eaten, young man. I don't believe you'll need persuading!"

Chapter Two

BACK IN THE KITCHEN, Gom, shivering, chafed his arms. It was cool under the thick stone walls. Cold, even. Harga banked up the fire, made hot oatmeal and apricots; warmed honey cakes and butter, and brewed strong black tea. And all, much to Gom's great disappointment, in the regular way, at the fire with pans and plates, and no sign of any spell.

"Tell me," she said. "I want to know about your brothers and sisters. Full half of them are married now with families, I understand."

Gom looked at her, surprised. "You don't know?"

"How can I, with me here and them there, Gom? Wizards are only people. We can't be everywhere, see everything."

"Not even my journeying?"

Harga reached over the table and took his hands, looking into his face. "That I'll speak of later. But for the rest, I did look in on you from time to time. Let me see. I saw you once by the creek, with a little green tree frog. On your tenth birthday. I saw you when you found the gold. And when you spoke to Mandrik. I had planned that for you, you know."

Gom nodded. Mandrik had told him that, after the rune's "humming" had steered him to the hermit and the gold his waking dreams had shown him.

Of course! "It was the rune, wasn't it?" Whenever it hummed, Harga had been close in her mysterious way. His heart contracted. All those times he'd fancied he heard it: at Stig's grave it had actually sung at last, clear and true. "When Father died . . ."

She squeezed his hands. "I watched you bury him, and kept wake with you by the fire."

Gom's eyes pricked with tears. "And we sang together, you and I that last time. I thought, when the rune sang—I hoped so."

Harga patted his hands, let them go, and picked up the teapot.

Gom watched her tip the pot to his cup. "But you knew what was to happen after." He grabbed his staff, wagged the sparrow at her. "You came to life in the bear cave. You gave me the riddle. You had to know about Katak. That I'd meet Ganash." If she didn't, then reason was out the window, and nothing made sense.

She set down the pot. "Some things I can foretell," she said. "Not everything."

"Oh." The notion stole into his mind again, he couldn't help it, and the insidious resentment, that she must have known, and knowing, that throughout she had made no move to protect her rune, or to save him from danger, and hurt, and even close brushes with death.

"Gom, Gom, you're pressing me." Harga continued to shake her head, her eyes on the blue-and-white checkered tablecloth. Then she looked up. "You judge wizards to be altogether too powerful and all-seeing. The only way I could help you was through the rune. Now think: was there ever a time when you called upon it and went unanswered?"

Gom hung his head, the color rising in his face. There had been one, after he'd flung the rune from him in rage. He looked up uncomfortably. "I didn't really mean," he began, but Harga cut in briskly.

"It's forgotten. You know, I've so looked forward to this meal. Now, tell me about everybody. Poor Horvin, I know he took my going ill."

Horvin? Gom made a face. He was not at all inclined to talk about Horvin, his bully brother.

"Yes, I saw him take the rune," Harga said, and added with a smile, "and how sorry he was for it afterward! But, you know, he was such a dear little boy when he was small."

Gom clamped his mouth shut. He couldn't imagine Horvin ever being small, or "dear."

"You see," Harga said gently, "he clung to me more than the rest. He needed me so. He wept bitterly after I left. It broke my heart to see it."

Silence. Clearly Harga was not inclined to talk about Gom's journey, or his struggle with Katak right now. "Tell me," Gom said, giving in, "how you found Windy Mountain, and how you met Father. He could never tell the tale with a straight face."

Harga thought a little bit, then, smiling once more, she told Gom what he asked, then more about life before he was born: not only of how she'd met and married Stig, but how they'd scraped along with their ever-increasing family, the nine dear children who'd been born, one after the other, every one the image of Stig, Harga said. Her eyes softened, and her voice grew warm and dreamy, until Gom began to feel jealous.

"I was the one you were after, Father said."

Harga sighed. "Aye. You were my only aim, in the beginning. The idea was to have a child, leave him, or her, safely out of the way with the father, and to be off again." She handed him his bowl of oatmeal. "But I reckoned without Stig. Such a wonderful man. And all my lovely children. I hadn't dreamed they'd prove so dear to me." She looked away.

"You had to leave," Gom declared stoutly, quite forgetting his recent resentment. "Ganash said."

His words brought her around again. "Aye. And you guessed why this very day: why you must be born, why I had to leave you behind on Windy Mountain."

Katak, thought Gom. *You have overcome yet you have not destroyed me. . . .* He shuddered. Katak was locked under the Deep Sound by his own evil spell, but riddle and dream had told him that it was not yet over. Whatever evil Katak represented still threatened Ulm, and Gom's fate was somehow bound up in it. "What's to do now?" he asked, venturing to touch on the matter at last.

"A very great deal, young man." Harga took up her oatmeal spoon, pointed it at him. "First, I must begin to teach you the magic arts."

Gom leaned forward eagerly. "When do we start?"

His mother smiled. "Ask me tonight, after supper," she said. And added over his rising excitement, "As for now, the sun is shining. We shall eat, then go outside—"

"But you said—"

"—and keep Stormfleet company in the garden."

They walked the sandy shore in the afternoon sun, then retreated into the orchard to cool off. Stormfleet stood by contentedly, ears cocked, tail swishing, cropping grass.

Gom could scarcely contain his impatience. His mind kept wandering back to Harga's words. That very night he would begin the life of a wizard. Would it take long to learn the magic arts? They were far harder even than an apothecary's, that he'd learned from Carrick. Gom's brows came together. Stig had told him many times what a quick mind he had, and so had Mandrik. But as yet he could neither read nor write.

"Gom?" Harga was watching him curiously.

"Sorry, Mother."

"Sing me a song."

Gom smiled with pleasure at the request, for he loved singing. "I sang last night, Mother, and the strangest creatures came to listen: big, shaggy they were, like bears, only they wore antlers."

"The *Faramors?*" Harga looked impressed. "You must have been in good voice. What happened?"

"They stood at the edge of the clearing, just swaying with the music. When I stopped, they waited, so I sang everything twice over, and after that, they went away. Who are these Faramors?"

"Ancient creatures of this forest. Having no gift of sound themselves they are drawn to music. Twice over, you say? They'll be in your debt forever—as your poor mother hopes to be if you'll but sing for her!"

Gom sang, one song after another, all the old favorites, finishing with "The Finch and the Sparrow": Harga's words, Stig's tune. At its close, when sparrow in his plain brown plumage flew away, leaving the gaudy finch caged in, Harga, laughing fondly, reached for Gom and held him tight. "We're two of a kind, you and I. Two of a kind. We're in no danger of gilded prison!"

Gom's heart swelled at the comparison. But on second thought, he pulled back and looked Harga severely in the eye. "Father thought you the most beautiful and wonderful Wife in the world."

"As I think you a son, no less. Yet you must admit not everyone sees us thus."

"Just those who count, eh, Mother?"

"Exactly." She sighed. "Did your father ever sing you his 'Song of the Hearth'?"

Song of the Hearth? Gom shook his head. He'd never heard of it.

"He made it just for me," Harga said.

A song of Stig's that Gom didn't know? "Sing it, Mother."

She shook her head. "I sing like a mallard."

Gom looked at her earnestly. "Please."

"Well, don't say I didn't warn you," she said, and began to sing.

> Walking home at twilight,
> through the misty mountain air,
> High above a darkling world,
> without a soul to care;
> See a light shine from my door,
> a shadow waiting there:
> Wife, who came in mystery, my lonely life to share!

> Climbing home at twilight,
> up a winding mountain path,
> To the sound of laughter,
> and the warmth of open hearth,
> Loving arms embrace me,
> children gather round my chair:
> Wife, you came in mystery, a joyous life to share.

When she was done, there was silence for a while. Then Gom sighed. "It was beautiful. And you sang fine well."

Harga wiped her eyes. "Tell me some more about the family, Gom."

Gom did so, telling mostly of Hilsa and Stok, to whom he'd been the closest, his eldest brother and sister who'd been second father and mother to the rest of the family after Harga left. Gom told about Stok's job with Maister Craw, the greengrocer. His growing family. About Hilsa's garden, her growing family, little Gudry, and the rest.

Harga sighed. "Fancy. Hilsa with her own children!" She stared off into space. "Such a good mother she must be. I wish . . ." She blew her nose loudly. "And that Gudry! He's tall as you already, you say, Gom?"

The shadows lengthened.

At last Harga touched on his journey. "Tell me how it all fell out, right from when you left home. But ask me no questions, please."

Gom told her how he'd left the Mountain, about his dream of sparrow and bear. Harga smiled then, and nodded, signaling that at least the riddle had been intended. But as he told of the skull-bird's attack, how he'd almost fallen to his death down the Bluff, her face grew grim. Quickly, he went on to tell how Hort and Mudge had nursed him well again, while glossing over the time he'd hurled the rune from him in pain and defiance.

Harga leaned forward, the rune swinging out from her chest. And as Gom spoke on, he watched her hand close about it, just as his had done all his life until that day. She must have missed it, too, he thought.

He told her how Zamul had stolen the rune and taken it to the Northern Sound. How Gom had followed him. About his meeting with Ganash, how with the rune regained, he'd set the kundalara free and shut Katak in his place. He paused, noting his mother's face, tight lips, deep furrow between her brows.

"Did I do well, Mother?"

Her face softened. "Better than I can say. Better than you can dream, Gom. Indeed, had you not done thus, you and I would not be sitting here together under the sun, for there would be no you, no me, no sun at all. But please—continue."

Puzzled, but pleased at his mother's praise—even though he'd prompted it—Gom went on to say how he'd gone south with Carrick the tinker to The Jolly Fisherman in Pen'langoth. How Zamul the conjuror had pursued him in Katak's stead, seeking to retrieve the rune for his master. How Gom, in fleeing Zamul, had outwitted the solahinn on the High Vargue and how he and Stormfleet had escaped. Rising to the crux of his tale, he told how Zamul in skull-bird shape had snatched the rune and fallen, and how, as the solahinn had closed in on horse and rider, Gom, in his extremity had cried "I am the seed!" At which, Harga's power had plucked them from the horsemen's whips and into that magic wood.

Harga listened, silent, while the shadows deepened, softening her face, veiling it in mystery. Whatever she already knew, she neither stopped him, nor asked questions, but let him talk on.

And as Gom did so, he breathed out much of his anger and resentment and fear and mistrust of Harga. When finally he fell silent, he leaned back against an apple tree, closed his eyes and listened to peaceful lake sounds, the drone of evening wings, and the idle waft of Wind.

Stormfleet, standing beside them, shook clouds of tiny insects from about his head. The sun went down behind the holly, stars lit up above the afterglow, and fireflies winked among the trees like tiny sparks.

Harga stood up, stretched. "Let's go pick supper," she said. "I have rare sweet carrots for a certain brave horse." She turned to Gom. "The business between you two in that camp I had no hand in. You and Stormfleet worked your own salvation there."

Gom patted Stormfleet's neck, pleased and proud: his own true friend, of his own making.

The three of them ambled about the vegetable beds, while Gom chose what they would eat: potatoes, lettuce, a cucumber long as Gom's arm, large ripe tomatoes, green beans, and . . . Gom pointed to fat green peapods on the vine.

Harga handed Gom a large wicker basket. "Pick what you want, but whistle over the peas, or we'll never be done! As for you, Stormfleet—" Harga pulled a bunch of carrots whose bright flesh glowed in the twilight. "Here."

While Gom picked the supper, feeling a healthy growing hunger in his belly, Harga led Stormfleet to the dairy, filled a pail with oats, and spread a bale of hay. Then Gom and Stormfleet stood by while Harga milked Jilly. When she was done, it was dark.

They bade Stormfleet good night and went indoors, Gom toting the loaded supper basket; Harga, a crock of frothy milk that she set to chill in a pantry off the hall.

While Harga toasted crispbread, Gom washed and tossed

the salad. Together they laid the table, then Harga set about making potato and parsley broth. Gom sighed happily. What a pleasure it was, to be about these homely chores. It certainly made one feel secure and comfortable, as in the old days with Stig. Although . . . it did seem like a deal of effort, when a fingersnap could pluck the meal from nowhere: toasted, tossed, and warmed, entire.

"I know by your face what you're thinking." Harga held up her wooden ladle. "Tell me, son of a woodcutter: how long was this in the making?"

Gom frowned. An hour, two, he almost said. Then he understood. It was not just a question of the ladle, but of the wood from which it was made. It took some years for even a quick jack pine to grow large enough to be of any consequence. A good woodcutter tended his forest carefully, cropping bad timber, nurturing the good, letting slow time do its work. Only a fool would hack and chop willy-nilly, for very soon, he'd waste his livelihood.

Magic must take no less time and effort to make and store, and likewise was not to be squandered on trifles.

Smiling now, Harga stirred.

Gom plucked up his courage. "Tonight—"

"All in good time." His mother kept her eye on the pot.

"It's tonight already," he said, looking to the darkened window.

"Not till after supper, it's not," she said.

Chapter Three

A T LAST, the dishes done and put away, and the fire banked up, Gom climbed the second stair, Harga going before him, carrying a lamp. At the sight of her back outlined against the lantern's glow, Gom remembered the false Harga under Great Krugk, evil image conjured up by Katak. When Gom had run to that one, she had raised the lamp to ward him off. "You think your mother would treat you thus?" Ganash had told him. "Young one, just you wait. When at last you meet with Harga, you will know the difference."

Harga's light going before him, Gom topped the stair and stepped out into his mother's workshop at last.

A long, low cavern, it curved off into darkness, running, so Harga said, almost the length of the hollow cliff. Gom advanced slowly in her wake, his eyes everywhere. High stone benches stood about haphazardly, stacked with sealed glass jars, and dishes, and boxes of all sizes; ironbound, some padlocked—from whom? Here and there lay heaps of gemstones, and large lumps of rock like coal shot with glowing golden veins.

Along the wall lay parchment scrolls, and piles of other objects that Gom had never seen. Not on Windy Mountain, not in Hort and Mudge's house; not in any place. But he'd heard speak of them, and he knew what they were.

He stopped, picked one up, almost dropped its unexpected weight. "It's a book."

"Aye, Gom," Harga said. "Go on, open it."

The covers were of wood, leather-bound, and hinged in brass. Gom lifted back the top cover, slowly turned the parchment leaves, while Harga held up the lamp for him to see. The pages were closely worked in neat, fine script. *Writing.* Gom eyed the markings intently. He wanted so badly to know, to understand the meaning of those spidery lines.

"Did you do this, Mother?"

"Aye," Harga said. "Wizards compile their own books. They make their own magic, you see, and store the secrets in those parchment pages. When you're a wizard, you'll do the same."

He hung his head. "I cannot read or write."

Harga smiled. "Not yet, maybe. But I'm sure you'll be doing both with ease before the year's end—and then you'll wish you did not, for I'll have you reading these books, every last one."

He pointed to the top of the first page. "What does that say?"

Harga set down the lamp on a nearby small wooden chest of drawers carved with leaves and fruit and moons and stars, and leaned over.

"It says, 'Compendium of Cardinal Remedies and Transformations.' "

"What's that?"

"A collection of spells for changing one thing into another. In it I've listed which stones or leaves or roots I need for which spell, together with their qualities, and the most effective admixtures for different cases."

Spells! Gom closed the book and replaced it carefully on the pile. *Compendium, admixtures:* it sounded very complicated. The books were all different colors, wine red, and green, and brown. He noticed farther down the wall several stacks of identically bound volumes in blue, some of them quite dusty and dark with age. "What are those?"

"My chronicles."

"Chronicles?"

"The record, if you like, of my life experience from the time I became a wizard."

Gom picked up one of the volumes. "Are we in your chronicles?" His father, his brothers and sisters, all the folk on Windy Mountain.

"Oh, yes, Gom. Of course."

Gom opened the book he was holding. "In here?"

Harga inspected the gilded symbols embossed on the cover's spine. "No." She looked along the wall. "I can't see those particular volumes offhand. We'll look later, maybe, and read some." She smiled at him. "We have plenty of time, now, you and I." She took up the lamp to move on.

But Gom, unwilling to give up the book, turned the pages over, yellowed leaves covered in the same close, neat hand. He couldn't wait another minute. "Read me some—now?"

Harga sighed. "Pick a page, any page."

Gom shut the heavy book, then let it fall open in his open palms. "Here," he said.

Harga leaned over, then drew in her breath sharply, staring down at the open page. "Of all the things . . ."

"Why, what is it, Mother?" She looked shaken. Had

he done something wrong? To his astonishment, she laughed.

"You cannot read, and yet you have found my very first mention of you. Here, give it here." She took the heavy book from him but did not begin to read at once. For a long minute, she scanned the page, her smile fading. When she did speak, her voice was low and serious.

". . . I only can defend Ulm from destruction. And yet this charge is too great for me alone. But to whom can I turn? Only Tolasin, and he is old. I have been thinking: I myself could have a child, a special child as I would bear by the right man. A child to share this task so that, should I come to grief, Ulm will not be left totally without defense. Yes, a secret child, left to grow under the protection and influence of gentle father and native soil, and of my own precious magic rune-stone. A child whose gifts the rune shall enhance, and whose inner senses it shall most finely attune. And under the rune's enchantment, the child shall grow slowly and slowly, like heart of oak, not counting the years as others. A risk, to leave this store of much of my greatest magic with one so young and unaware, but that I must take. Then, when the time is right, I'll test the child's mettle, demanding the return of my stone. If all goes well, and the child succeeds in bringing me my rune, then I shall teach that child all I know, sharing all my magic treasures for the sake of Ulm. . . ." She looked up, her eyes bright. "And here you are. My little tool to save the world: tested, tempered, proven by the water and the fire." Her smile twisted. "Oh, Gom." She set down the chronicle, and folded him to her, rocking him to and fro.

Stig had been right; Ganash had spoken true, just as Gom had known in his better moments. . . . *should I come to grief, Ulm will not be left totally without defense* . . . Smitten by the weight of those words, Gom put his arms about his mother's middle and held on. "What does it mean?" he mumbled.

But Harga did not answer him. Presently, she stood him out at arm's length. "We must move along. Time is passing," she said, and, taking up the lamp now, she made to go down the chamber. Beside the lamp stood a large blue globe on a dull brass spindle. Gom reached out, touched it, recoiled as the ball rolled under his palm. Had he broken it? "What is it?"

"This?" Harga set it spinning faster. "It's Ulm."

"Ulm?" *Ulm?* Gom drew out Carrick's map, spread it beside the globe. Flat brown parchment and round blue globe looked nothing like.

Harga was staring fixedly at the spinning thing, gone off into her own thought. Only as it slowed did she answer him. "They say Ulm's flat. It's not: it's round, and bigger than your tinker knows. That map covers less than one fourth this globe. See." Harga stopped the spinning sphere, then rolled it slowly until a large green-brown patch on the upper hemisphere came into view. Gom looked keenly from map to sphere, comparing. The patch was something like the Ulm of Carrick's map, but much longer from north to south. And it was colored various greens and browns, with stretches of white to the north in the Far Fjords, red dots and yellow patches down in the southwest. The rest of the globe was blue.

"The white is snow," Harga said. "The red, volcano and thermal land. See, here by the Dread Shore." She drew her finger along the southwestern edge of the continent.

"Volcano? Thermal?" Gom had never heard of either word.

"Volcanoes are mountains of fire. When that fire boils close to the surface you get thermal land." Harga's eyes gleamed. "I've seen places where boiling water shoots plumes of steam high into the air—those plumes are called geysers—and great valleys of boiling mud. The red"—she tapped the globe—"marks the volcanoes; the yellow, the mud. The blue, of course, is ocean, which, as you can clearly see"—she turned the globe on—"covers most of Ulm." Harga looked up. "There are islands in the southern hemisphere, but they're small and scattered, and since I don't know exactly where they lie, I haven't marked them in."

Islands! "Any people?"

"A few, so the gulls tell me, but those folk never travel far from land. The oceans are vast and dangerous. And those who've set out from our shores in big boats have either never gotten far—or failed to return."

"Do others know all this besides you?"

"A few other wizards know a little, and little it is, they lacking good gull gossip."

Gom looked from globe to map, still comparing. On Carrick's map, the southern Shore, a smooth, unbroken line with no sign of Dread Shore to the west, or the volcanoes that Harga had spoken of.

"No tinker or peddler goes that far south. There is no reason, for few men live that way," Harga said. "It's too hot down there, too uncomfortable and unhealthy for most folk. And dangerous—" She tapped the bright red dots on her globe.

"Do you go down there, Mother?" Gom asked.

Harga went down the chamber a little way, fetched back bits of yellow powdery rock, some of them crumbling in her hand. "I go for these. With them I make much powerful magic. When my store is used up, I shall fetch more."

Gom eyed the rocks with interest. "May I go with you?"

Harga smiled. "I hope so."

"Doesn't anyone at all live down there?"

Harga touched a narrow peninsula to the far west where lay clustered the greatest concentration of red dots. "Here, west of the Dread Shore you'll find a strange folk. That's the hottest region of all. Throughout their land are geysers, and pools they boil potatoes in. It's a terrible place for us cool climate people. The air peels the skin off your face, and it stinks of rotten eggs—the sulfur, you see." She held the stones under his nose.

Gom snapped his head back in distaste, recognizing the smell at once.

Sulfur! It stank of Ganash on the point of becoming mangatla-aczai. "Would that be what dragon smells of?"

"Aye." Harga shot him a quick look. "Of course, you'd know. The air down there is full of it, you can't escape it."

"Do you have dealings with that folk?"

"Not as a wizard. They have their own, which is unusual, for the wizards of the Guild belong to no one, but go wherever they are called. Anyhow, these folk have what they call the *Onder.* More than a wizard, he is also their king. Because of this, they choose him in a most remarkable way."

"Oh?"

Harga set the stones down. "They have a volcanic bridge, no wider than your foot, arcing like a rainbow high over boiling mud. When the old Onder dies, his would-be successor must walk that bridge to the other side."

"Doesn't sound so bad." Gom had trodden stone bridges narrow as that many times under Windy Mountain, over dizzy crevasses and in pitch darkness.

"Oh?" Harga pursed her mouth. "I'm sure you'd have no trouble climbing underground, Gom. Or even up a cliff. But you might find taking such an airy walk another matter. As for those folk, few elect to try, and fewer succeed. Imagine inching your way into the sky over choking fumes, with nothing to hold on to if you should wobble, and no room to turn back if you would change your mind."

"They sound a hard, cruel folk."

"Perhaps. But walking that bridge tests the candidate's will to rule the self—that they demand above all of one who would wield great power over them for life. To that one only will they entrust the fate of the tribe."

"I see—I think," Gom said slowly. Hadn't Harga herself tested him, her own son, thus, in having him bring her the rune? That was for a purpose, a very important one, to do with saving Ulm, no less. Curbing his impatience to know more, he turned his eye farther north and eastward to the High Vargue, that vast plain over which the solahinn hunted wild horse endlessly: Stormfleet's birthplace, to which the cito might never safely return.

On Carrick's map, there was no sea to the east, the High Vargue being, so the tinker had said, the eastern end of the world. Curiously, Gom turned the globe to compare, and looked up, puzzled. No coastline here, either; the land merged with sea as though wet colors had run. "Mother?"

"Neither I nor gull nor any living creature on Ulm has clearly seen the land beyond the Vargue."

"There *is* more there, then?"

Harga pulled her shawl about her and firmly took up the lamp. "I don't know about you," she said, "but I'm cold standing here. Let's go and light the stove." She drew him to the far end of the chamber where two armchairs stood side by side with a little table in between. In front of them was a dusty stove embossed with clustered grapes and vine leaves, and capped with a chimney running up into the vaulted roof.

She sat Gom down in one of the armchairs. Then, taking out a flint, she struck the tinder already laid in the stove, and bright blue flames shot up the flue. Replacing the stove lid, she threw herself into the other armchair and held out her hands to warm.

Gom watched her movements closely. Harga had suddenly gone like Sessery, avoiding his last question, he was sure of it. He pressed her again. "How can you know there's more land beyond the Vargue if no one has seen it?"

"I have seen something of what lies there—not a lot, but some."

"Why only 'some'? Why hasn't anyone else? Surely, if you walked east—"

Harga smiled. "Walk all you like, you'd only get lost in the mist."

"What mist?"

"The magic mist the Spinrathe use to hide their presence there." She turned toward him. "I've been asked to say nothing of them until after you have met with one."

The backs of Gom's hands tingled. "When?"

"This very night."

"Here?"

"We go there."

"Beyond the Vargue?" More magic! Another wonderful whirlwind like the one that had plucked him from that plain and set him down in the Dunderfosse?

"In a manner of speaking."

At her solemn face, his excitement turned flat. "It's to do with Katak."

"Partly. Katak and the Spinrathe are of the same place."

"He's one of them?"

Harga looked annoyed. "Gom, bears and foxes live on Ulm, but that doesn't make you one."

Gom looked down, abashed for a moment, then he rallied. "How could they and Katak live so long on Ulm without folk knowing?"

"Who said they did?"

Gom gazed at her blankly.

"They don't dwell east of the Vargue," she went on. "Nor on Ulm at all."

His flesh pricking, Gom glanced down the room, to the globe's solid bulk, to its shadow wavering on the wall. "Where, then?"

"The Spinrathe live among the stars."

A coal shifted, collapsed, jumping him in his skin.

Harga leapt up. "Dear, dear! It's almost time and we're not ready!" She produced a small crystal sphere big as Gom's fist and set it on the table.

"When that flashes, we go," she said.

"This is magic?"

"Indeed," Harga said, her dark eyes gleaming.

"How do we get there?"

Harga fixed her eyes on the crystal globe. "We go, but we don't go, in a manner of speaking."

"How, in a manner of speaking?"

"We travel in mind only. But being there will seem so real that you'll doubt my word. Yet all the time our bodies will be here, before the stove."

Gom's face cleared. He understood now. "Like in a waking dream."

Harga nodded vigorously. "Yes, only much more so. You see—"

There came a brilliant flash, making Gom blink, then the globe went dark again.

"It's time," Harga said. "Take my hand."

Even as she said that, the sphere began to glow, brighter and brighter. Harga placed her free hand over the brightness and in that same instant Gom felt a sort of shimmering through his whole body.

"Don't be afraid," Harga said. "You'll come to no harm, I promise."

"I'm not afraid," he wanted to say, but just then the crystal flared up a second time, and he and Harga and everything vanished in a shower of golden sparks.

Chapter Four

THE TINGLING, the sparking passed. Gom became aware of light on his eyelids. Also that he was still holding tightly to Harga's hand. How long they had been thus he had no idea. He had no sense of time passing at all.

Harga gently disengaged herself. "We're here."

Gom opened his eyes onto thick milky haze. He breathed it up, smelled moist earth and moss. Seemed real. He scuffed the dirt under his boots. Felt real. Just as Harga had said, he'd swear he really was here, between the High Vargue and the eastern ocean, off the edge of Carrick's map, hundreds of miles from the Dunderfosse, and not still sitting by Harga's stove.

Harga was eyeing him with amusement, but didn't say, I told you so.

Gom became aware of an unnatural silence: no sound of bird, of wind, of anything. He cleared his throat, and the sound came out thin and without echo. "What now?"

"We wait for Jastra," Harga said.

Jastra? That must be the Spinrathe. Gom peered through the mist, expecting to see at any moment this Jastra looming out of it to greet them. Keeping close to Harga, Gom crossed his arms tight over his chest, although it wasn't cold. And took to wondering what manner of person this was, who lived beyond the stars.

"Ha," Harga said suddenly. "It looks as though we're to go up."

The mist divided, forming a narrow gap, clear path through the thick white vapor. And there before them, without pillar, post, or handrail, a shining crystal stair curved up into the heights. They were to climb that? Some test of nerve! "Like the Onder's bridge," he murmured.

"Yes. Save there's no boiling mud below it, nor can you fall, since you're not here in body, remember that. Come on, keep close." Harga set her foot on the bottom step, invisible in the mist but for its shine, so that it looked as though Harga was holding her foot in the air.

Gom, his middle churning, remembered Harga's warning about the Onder's bridge. She'd been right. The idea of climbing that stair bothered him.

Above his head by now, Harga stopped, looking down. "Gom?"

He started up. One step, two. The stair was narrow, scarcely wider than his two feet. The toe of his boot caught the edge of a step with a loud *crrk,* and his middle churned some more.

Gom went higher. Looking down, he saw only a faint gleam of light on the edge of each step, curving away toward the ground. He looked up, saw his mother's back fading into the mist.

"Harga."

Gom almost fell as the voice, a man's, sounded close by.

Harga stopped. "Jastra?" She half glanced back to Gom, uncertainly.

"Go back, Harga. Let the boy come on alone."

"Alone?" Harga looked shocked. "But, Jastra, you said—"

"Please."

She turned about with great care on her narrow step and looked down, her face set. "Don't be afraid, Gom. Remember that, whatever happens, you're not really here, but still at home, sitting with me by the stove." She glanced up again, then leaned down, frowning slightly. "I hadn't reckoned—"

She vanished.

"Mother!" Gom teetered, snatched for a nonexistent rail and almost fell—how far? He began to tremble. Slowly, fearfully, he lowered himself and sat, unable to move another step on that dizzy sky bridge, up or down.

Let the boy come on alone . . .

He sought the rune, it wasn't there.

Let the boy come on alone . . .

How could this Jastra do such a cruel thing! He took a deep breath to shout—a mistake, for it only set his head spinning, and dark flecks flowering silently before him. Carefully, Gom let the breath out.

But his anger grew, mixed with fear. This Jastra had dismissed his mother, and when she'd delayed, had plucked her from the stair. Was he more powerful than she? It seemed like it, and yet she'd clearly trusted him, had urged Gom not to fear. He stood up cautiously. He must go on. The appeal in her eyes had been quite plain.

But this stair—how high was it? How much farther must he climb into the mist? His head began to spin again. Air wafted against his ears like puffs of wind. He swayed, caught his balance. *What if he lost consciousness?* Gom summoned all his nerve, and went on up with new resolve.

Suddenly the stair ended, and wide crystal floor was

under him, solid, and thick, like ice on a winter pond. A narrow passage stretched before him, a glass tunnel lit with milky light. All at once, a single high note shrilled, setting the air singing, making his skin prickle. The echoes died, leaving utter silence.

"Hello!" he shouted. No reply. Shrugging, he moved on, conscious of his boots' loud crunch in the quiet.

Reaching the end of the passage, Gom turned the corner, and halted in wonder. The space ahead was bounded by mist and filled with light. There were no walls, no roof, that he could see, only the glassy floor spreading out into the mist, and yet he sensed that he was *inside*.

In the center of that sky hall stood a tree. Ancient as any in the Dunderfosse, its trunk, wide as six men in a ring, soared up, up, up—Gom tilted his head back, squeezed his eyes shut against the dazzle—to what height he could not guess.

From the tree's base, roots thick as Gom's whole body curled out like serpents into round, crystal pools, each with a fountain that sent sprays of sparkling mist high into the air.

Gom approached, perplexed. Trees were of the soil. With each passing year, their roots thrust themselves deeper into the earth even as their branches reached to greater heights. So what was this ancient magnificence doing floating in the sky?

He leaned over the nearest fountain, trying vainly to judge its depth, then looked around, the puzzle growing. There was about it all—roots, pools, even tree trunk itself—altogether too much of a regular pattern. He fished in his back pocket, took out his little wooden seed box, set it down as marker by the fountain, then circled the base of the tree, pacing, counting, until he reached his starting place.

Yes, he nodded, picking up the box, stowing it away. Regular pattern indeed there was: twelve roots, and twelve fountains exactly twelve paces apart, in perfect circle around the tree. Surely no tree in all Ulm had such tidy roots. In fact—Gom looked the great trunk up and down. Not oak, not ash, not elm, or hickory. Not any tree of Ulm. Gom's eyes gleamed. The Spinrathe lived among the stars. Could this wonderful tree have come from out there?

His fingers itched to touch the golden bark. But something, he couldn't explain what, held him back. He tilted his head. Way up, he now could see, hazy branches curved out in graceful arc, bearing shiny oval leaves such as he had never seen before.

Looking up had not been wise. The dizziness was back. Truly, there was a strangeness in the air. Gom bent over bracing his hands on his knees, the dark gray patches bursting before his eyes, and this time, there was a faint humming in his head.

The giddiness passed, the dark patches disappeared. But the humming remained. A faint, musical humming, just as he'd often fancied *almost* had come from his mother's rune, with . . . the faint tinkle of bells.

He looked up, and straightened slowly.

Instead of the tree stood a shining crystal tower, broad like the tree, and soaring into the haze. Up and down inside its length ran fine silver wires that fizzed with tiny sparks. The glassy surface was pocked with small round holes in which tiny silver spheres jiggled about, making the bell sounds. And where branches had arched from the tree trunk sprang tufts of silver wires, nodding like delicate plumes, each tuft humming on a different note.

From the base of the tower, hollow glass tubes piped the wires out and down into pits of blue fire that flashed and flickered silently.

Gom stood still for quite a minute, totally entranced, then he stirred himself and called, "Hello?" then more loudly, "Hel-lo-ho!"

The feathery tufts danced wildly, and the little silver spheres pealed like a cartload of bells cascading down a hillside. Echoes made intricate counterpoint through the high, hollow space, then faded.

Without warning, the air trembled, and the whole tower shimmered, as though it were underwater. When the shimmering stopped the tower was gone and in its place the ancient tree reappeared, and its twelve roots, and their dancing fountains, and the air was filled with spray.

A beam of light suddenly shone from the heights of the tree, forming a pool of radiance on the floor before him, and in that pool the shape of a man began to form.

He was tall and lean, with strong jaw; broad, straight nose, and wide full mouth. His eyes were dark, deep-set, and deep-shadowed under the brilliant light; his black hair tipped with silver, and hanging in thick strands about his shoulders, was caught at the brow by a fine crystal band set with a clear stone big as a thrush's egg that flashed in the light.

The man looked tired, and, it seemed to Gom, sad, even dispirited. His dark gray tunic was stained as Gom's, and torn at the shoulder, and his black thigh boots were much scuffed and spattered with mud.

He bowed gravely. "Lord Jastra, Guardian of the Tamarith-awr-Bayon, greets you, Harga's son."

Lord Jastra? The man looked more bedraggled than any tinker or peddler Gom had met on the Pen'langoth road. "What do you want?" Gom demanded, then realizing how blunt that sounded, changed his tack before Jastra could reply. "My mother thought that we would be speaking all together."

Jastra closed his eyes in acknowledgment. "As we had planned. But things changed." The Spinrathe folded his arms. "You know why you are here?"

Gom hesitated. Those sharp eyes seemed to see right through him, made him feel small, and self-important, and foolish. He had a sudden notion he was here for this Jastra to look him over. And that somehow Ulm's fate was closely connected to this being. Jastra was beginning to frown. What should he say? "Katak, I think," he said quickly.

The frown remained. "How was your journey up the stair, young man?"

"I've known better," Gom retorted, then bit his tongue, but to his surprise, Jastra's face cleared.

"If you'd fallen, there'd have been no real harm, you know."

"So my mother claimed," Gom said, and added, he couldn't help it, for the man was still rattling him, "much comfort that was."

"And yet still you kept climbing," Jastra murmured. He sighed, and bent his head, his face looking suddenly haggard under the light beam. His form began to shimmer, to grow transparent. He looked up, squared his shoulders, and his shape steadied, grew solid again.

"Why—you're no more real than I am!" Gom cried. Jastra was here in much the same way as he and Harga had come by means of her crystal sphere. Except, perhaps, that Jastra's appearance seemed more difficult.

Jastra smiled. "True. You and I are worlds apart. Yet by the power of the Tamarith I come here in spirit just as you came here in spirit by virtue of your mother's power. And thus we may speak together awhile."

"What is *Tamarith?*"

"The Tree of Life."

Gom gestured behind him. "This is it?" The name sounded fitting for such a majestic thing.

"Yes, and no. The parent tree is in Bayon—my world. That yonder is a scion, yet real enough."

Gom was aware suddenly of the floor they were standing on, suspended high above the ground. "Is—is this place real?"

"It is. This place, and the tree, and the stair: they are all real, and will remain after we vanish. Only you and I are unreal. It is called *alamar:* I am alamar-Jastra."

"And I, alamar-Gom!"

Again, the quick pleasure in Jastra's face, just as swiftly gone. "Young man, this meeting is not a happy one. I need your mother, urgently."

Gom stared in dismay. "But we've only just—" he began, then looked up into the light beam arcing out from the heights of the tree. "How far?"

"To where I am."

"How—how long?"

Jastra looked grave. "It could be long."

Gom's middle went hollow. He tried to speak, couldn't.

"I am truly sorry," Jastra said. "Neither I nor Harga foresaw it. In fact, she still thinks that tomorrow you and she begin work together. But it is not to be."

"Why?" Gom demanded. "What do you want with her?"

Jastra thought a minute. "I'll let your mother tell you that."

"It's to do with Katak!"

"If only that were all!" Anger flashed in Jastra's face, was quickly controlled. "The cunning one slipped our line. Even your mother had no idea of his coming. Had he breached this stair, it would have been disaster for us, total destruction for Ulm." He dipped his head. "And you stopped him. A callow, untried boy."

Callow? Untried? Gom didn't know about that.

"Young man," Jastra went on, "I see now how right your mother's thinking was to have a child. Thanks to you, Katak stays locked in his own spell until we may safely destroy him. Which, I'm afraid, I can't yet do."

"Even with Harga's help?"

"Perhaps then, if I were to come to Ulm, and Harga and I stood together, combining our magic and our will. But know, young man, that there are two more like Katak loose among the Realms and it is more than I can do to contain them. That is why I cannot come, and why I call on your mother right now, for the struggle goes against us. Now this is the charge I lay upon you: while she is gone, you must work to become a wizard like Harga, as she intended."

Gom slowly shook his head. Who would teach him, if not Harga? He could not believe she was leaving him. Leaving *Ulm!* "Is there—danger for my mother?"

"There is danger for us all, including you, if we should fail to hold the line. If this realm fall, your world follows."

Ulm fall! Harga had spoken of it, and now Jastra. Gom could not imagine it. He recalled the deathly cold of Katak's touch, the evil of the hollow eyes. If Katak gained power over Ulm, it would mean the end of all ordinary living. Of Hilsa and Stok and Hort and Mudge, Carrick and Essie. Of fields and rustic festivals; of the wonderful lake cities. Of great Pen'langoth, the citadel, and the fishermen's quarter. Katak was cunning beyond measure. What if he somehow escaped his deep cave? What could Gom do about it? What did they expect of him? Panic stirred within him. Surely it took years to become a wizard?

"Do not be so anxious, Gom," Jastra said. "Go back to Harga, take your leave—and do not make it hard on her. You cannot know how deeply she loves you, or how proud she is of you, how much faith she has in you. Listen to her: she'll find you a mentor. Take him, study well, and remember that your world, my world, nay all the Seven Realms may one day depend on the part that we each play." He raised his hand. "Until we speak again, farewell."

Mentor? Seven Realms? Gom's head was reeling. Even so, he glanced around nervously. "I'm to go back down there?"

Jastra's mouth twitched. "I'll speed you. Ready?"

"Wait." Gom pointed. "You called the Tamarith the Tree of Life."

Jastra nodded. *Tamarith-awr-Bayon:* The Tree of Life out of Bayon."

"And this one is just like it?"

"Indeed. It is a true scion, as I said."

"A tree? That's all it is?"

Jastra's face became watchful. "What do you mean, *all?*"

Gom hesitated, then jumped in. "Before you arrived, I saw something else, only for a second, but I saw it, I'm sure."

The dark eyes gleamed. "And what was that?"

"A great glass column set with silver wires that hummed, and little bouncing spheres that sounded like bells. And—" Gom pointed to the misty fountains. "—pools of bright blue flashing fire."

The Spinrathen lord looked startled, even shocked.

"It was certainly most strange," Gom went on, pressing his advantage.

But Jastra, recovering, only nodded, his face expressionless. "Mist and light can play such tricks," he said. "Time to go. Stand fast."

Before he knew it, Gom's head began to turn. If not by stair, how would he go back? was his last conscious thought.

Gom opened his eyes. He was curled up in the armchair before the stove. How he had gotten there he couldn't remember. But then, he reminded himself, he hadn't really been away! Harga slumped opposite, eyes closed, lips parted.

"Mother?" he called softly. She didn't move, or give any sign that she was aware. He leaned over the table that divided them, and the crystal sphere, still glowing. "Mother?"

Still no response. Gom glanced to the clustered windows. Dark, as ever, giving no idea how long they had been sitting there, or what time it was.

Images of his journey came back like a remembered dream. Impressions of height, space, mist, the dizzy stair. And the Tamarith, Tree of Life—crystal pillar that he was sure he hadn't been supposed to see. Harga must be there still, in that strange place, talking with Jastra, planning her departure. He eyed her bleakly. Why, he might never see her again, never, never—

He turned away. The last of his lifelong resentment was gone. Until now, he'd still thought of her as all-powerful, a magician-puppeteer, pulling strings to make him dance. Whatever was happening, Harga was in its grip no less than he, no more able than he to direct the outcome. Gom closed his eyes, saw her face on the stair; the shock, the distress, the concern for him.

He mustn't show how much he minded. He must remember what Jastra had said about doing his part, and how proud Harga was of him. When Harga came back to herself, she'd need him to be brave, and understanding: a good obedient son.

A shiver seized him. The air was cold; the fire had burned low. He shifted in his chair, found that his left leg had gone quite numb under him. He stood, rubbed his calf, starting pins and needles up and down. Then he raked the ashes, put more wood on the stove.

Harga looked so peaceful, showing nothing of what must be going on between her and Jastra. Gom told himself that she wasn't having a pleasant time of it, either. She'd been so looking forward to their work to-gether in that room too.

He leaned over, touched her cheek with the back of

his fingers. Cold. He pulled her shawl about her shoulders, tucked the corners under her hands.

Flames spurted from the new-caught wood, fire crawled greedily over its surface, turning gold to black, exploding loud sparks up the chimney.

Gom climbed into his own armchair and leaned back. Harga going away! He squeezed up his face, let out a tight, muffled sound, half misery, half pain. Then pulling himself up, he folded his hands in his lap, fixed his eyes on his mother's small form, and waited for her to awake.

Chapter Five

GOM AWOKE in the armchair, a blue blanket
tucked around him. The stove was barely warm,
and Harga's seat was empty. Bright sunlight
through the eastern wall poked the chilly air, set dust
motes swirling.

He stood, stretched, folded the blanket, and went
downstairs, the smell of new-baked oatcake strong
upon him.

"Ah!" Harga looked up from the hearth, and, smiling,
turned her cheek for a kiss. "Sit. Tea's made." She set
the loaded plate of oatcakes on the table. "I've milked
Jilly, and given Stormfleet fresh hay. He sends you a
bright good morning." She eyed the stacked plate doubtfully. "Perhaps I should have baked more," she said.

But after only one cake, Gom's appetite was gone.
"When do you leave?"

Harga blinked. "I begin to see what folk mean when
they call me . . . direct. Blunt as two old blades, we
are—but—refreshing, if you can take it!" She poured
the tea. "Tomorrow at sunrise you and I must part."

Tomorrow! Gom stared, he couldn't help it. *Tomorrow!*

"Gom, you know I have no choice."

Silence.

"I know nothing," he declared at last, his newfound

understanding fleeing out the window. "You only tell me: do this, go there."

"Gom."

He snatched another cake, bit into it savagely. *Gom*, he mimicked inwardly. It was all very well for Harga. He stared miserably at the cake on his plate, the large, round hole where he'd taken a bite. He wanted to jump up and rush around and beg her not to go away. And at the same time tell her calmly to go and not to worry about him; that he understood, and would obey, like the good son he'd resolved to be. But with all these different urges boiling around inside him, each fighting for victory, he could only sit stiff as old wood, looking resentful, even hostile.

Harga got up, walked around the table to him. "Poor Gom, to have a wizard mother." Leaning over, she put her arms about him.

He closed his eyes, buried his head against her middle. "Sorry." The word was muffled in folds of blouse.

"There." Harga patted his back, then, sighing, released him, and returned to her chair. "Eat up. We have much to do before we take our ways."

Take our ways. It came like a stab. "You're going to Bayon?"

"No."

"Where, then?"

"To Jastra, to do my part. And you shall take your life in a fresh direction."

"Oh, Mother!"

"I know. We should be going up those stairs to start work this very minute." She fixed her eyes sadly on him.

"But we can't." When he didn't respond, she added sharply, "Gom, don't make it harder than it is."

Fine son you're turning out to be, Gom sneered. After all your brave resolutions. He was behaving badly, he knew, but every time he would have his tongue say one thing, his heart wagged it to say quite another.

"If you'd only tell me *why*," he said at last. Then, quickly, "Jastra said you'd do it."

"Yes," Harga said. "He would. Gom, you know I have to go away, that you must find yourself a master and learn the arts of magery. Isn't that enough?"

No, his chin said.

Harga took up her teacup, set it down again with a sigh. "Of course not." She got up, took down a jar of peppercorns from her spice shelf, and brought it back to the table. "Stars," she said, rattling the jar. "They're all much the same, yes?"

Gom eyed her doubtfully. Was this some test? "No-o. They're all different sizes and colors, and some are brighter than others."

Harga looked pleased. "Quite so, Gom. And now I'll tell you more: most of those stars are really suns, great sky furnaces like ours, but much farther away so that they look smaller, and we don't feel their heat. Others are worlds that shine only by reflected light. Like Ulm . . ." She cleared a space on the table, shook several peppercorns out onto the white cloth. She picked up one, held it between finger and thumb. ". . . and Bayon." She set the peppercorn down, then added more, spacing them out one by one like beads on a string, right across the table, until they counted seven.

"The Seven Realms," Gom breathed.

"Yes. And each is home to the Spinrathe. But Bayon was the first, and is still their prime world. And each of the other six is powered by the magic in Tamarith crystal." Harga cocked her head. "Jastra told me what you saw last night."

"So I did see true!" And the Tamarith was not tree at all, but crystal pillar. "Why have me see a tree?"

"Jastra didn't want to confuse you. He meant you to see only what you would expect to see. But he reckoned without you."

Didn't want me to see the Tamarith until he'd looked me over, more like, Gom thought, but kept that to himself. He pictured the wondrous crystal column suspended high above Ulm's eastern plains, frowning. "He called it the Tree of Life."

"That was no lie, Gom. The columns do look much like a tree trunk. And the crystals on the prime Tamarith, the Tamarith-awr-Bayon, actually live and grow. When they break a shaft off the prime Tamarith, the Tamarith grows it back. The offshoot then grows into a new Tamarith, then it stops, unable thereafter to replace lost crystals. Yet it stays alive and 'connected' with its parent right across the heavens. That is how all the Realms have their Tamarith. By their magic the Spinrathe hear and see one another from afar—"

"As Jastra spoke with me! He called it alamar!"

"Yes. But there is greater magic still in the Tamariths: by means of those crystal pillars, they can travel from Realm to Realm."

"*Across the sky?* I don't understand, Mother."

Harga moved her finger from peppercorn to peppercorn, from the first in turn, all down the line. "From Bayon, they can pass by means of the Tamariths from one Realm to the next, through the star-gates one by one right out to the seventh and most distant one."

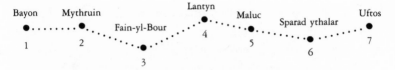

Bayon   Mythruin   Lantyn   Maluc   Uftos
                   Fain-yl-Bour   Sparad ythalar
1   2   3   4   5   6   7

"Star-gates?"

"That is what the Spinrathe call the Tamariths when they use them to pass from Realm to Realm."

Star-gates. Gom thought of Hilsa's white picket gate back on Windy Mountain leading from the street along the path lined with phlox and snapdragon, right up to her front door. Of Hort's farmhouse gate that swung out from the front yard toward the hills beyond. That crystal pillar—a gate?

Puzzled, Gom propped his elbows on the table, staring down at the neat line of peppercorns. Stars, strung out across the sky, folk passing across the starry skies as the swallows outside flew the summer air. He shook his head, trying to imagine it. Seven Realms, seven star-gates. Seven? He thought of the crystal stair leading to the tall shining column in the sky hall. He looked up. "The Tamarith I saw last night—that's a star-gate too!"

"Aye," Harga said grimly. "And that's the trouble."

"Trouble?" Gom sat up. "Is that why Katak came?"

"Yes. You see, the Seven Realms form a commonwealth, with Lord Jastra at the head. A while back, Lord

Karlvod, ruler of Maluc, got greedy." She tapped the fifth peppercorn. "He wanted Jastra's place—and the Tamarith-awr-Bayon. He started a long and subtle campaign to stir up strife and dissent, to break the commonwealth. He blazed a trail of chaos halfway to Bayon before anyone even suspected it."

"How?" Gom couldn't imagine anyone fooling Lord Jastra.

"Karlvod had a stroke of luck—for him. In Maluc's fens, he discovered three creatures that they call Spohr. These Spohr have no solid body of their own, nor any great intelligence, yet they can take the shape of anyone and anything, can enter the minds of others and bend them to their will—or, rather, Karlvod's. They—"

"Katak!" Hadn't Jastra mentioned that Katak was one of three?

"Yes, Katak, as Ganash named him. *Evil One.* Karlvod bound them to him, and taught them how to do his bidding."

Gom slapped the table, rattling the cups, bouncing the peppercorns. "So Katak isn't the real enemy after all—it's Karlvod!"

"Dear, the knife is just as deadly as the hand that throws it!"

He sat back. "So why the star-gate on Ulm, and why is Katak here?"

Harga looked up. "Prepare yourself. When Jastra found out what Karlvod was doing, he publicly broke the star lane between Bayon and the second Realm, sealing off Bayon to protect it." She set another peppercorn between the first and second, and out a ways, to form a triangle.

"But so that he could still go secretly to and fro, he built a buffer gate on what he was pleased to call 'a minor body off the main star lane.' "

"Ulm!"

"Yes. This secret buffer gate worked well for a long time while the struggle against Karlvod went on—and Karlvod did persist, even after Bayon was safely sealed off."

Gom leaned forward excitedly. "Karlvod found out about this star-gate, and sent Katak to find it, and to breach it from here!"

Harga dipped her head gravely. "That is so."

"But—" He frowned. . . . *disaster for us,* Jastra had said, *total destruction for Ulm* . . . "I can see that is bad for the Spinrathe, and for us if they bring their fight to our door. But 'total destruction'?"

"When Jastra installed that eighth gate on our world, he sealed it with many spells, all very strong. But the last spell was strongest, designed to hold should all else fail: should an enemy break those seals and breach the crystal stair, then the gate will self-destruct—and shatter all Ulm with it!"

Chapter Six

"SHATTER?" Out in the summer meadows small ripe puffballs popped their clouds of minute spores in the space of a minute, leaving dry and empty stalk. If Katak pierced the mist and climbed the crystal stair, then Ulm would vanish likewise, a dustcloud blowing on the winds—and Jastra would be its cause. "Our enemy's not Katak or Karlvod. It's Jastra!"

"Wait, Gom. When Jastra built this gate, there were no folk here. Ulm was just a blob of unremarkable dirt off his beaten sky track. He didn't know what it would grow into."

"Can't he change the spell, or simply take it off?"

"You think I didn't ask—nay, demand it? The spell is so powerful not even he can reverse it."

"Then he must tell Karlvod to leave the gate alone."

"He did. Karlvod thinks it another bluff."

Gom leaned back, his face set, thinking over all he'd learned: of star Realms, star-gates, and living crystals that grew like trees. And a buffer gate that might bring his world to a sudden end. He shook his head as though to clear it. "What if Katak gets out while you're away, and sets about finding magic power again?"

"How can he, Gom? He can't reach the sealstone from within the cave, and he's the only one who can reverse the stone's spell by touching it."

"I suppose so." Another thought occurred. "How did Katak get here?"

"Along the stellar winds. Having no body, the Spohr can travel through the heavens freely without harm."

"Then what's to stop the others from coming here?"

"I'd say they're too busy elsewhere. But even if Karlvod were to send them, that kind of travel takes long. Long enough for you to become a wizard, Gom." She picked up the peppercorns briskly and dropped them back into the jar. "So go about your business, work to do your part in this, we're counting on you." She restoppered the spice jar and returned it to its shelf.

"But how?" Gom's voice, rising, cracked. "How shall I learn magic now?"

"I've given that some thought." Harga sat down again, and calmly refilled her cup. "There are two or three wizards who might do for mentor."

Mentor. A stranger, who'd have Gom in his sole power for long enough. Gom had suffered a lifetime of unkindness from folk who couldn't, wouldn't understand him. He'd thought to have left them behind on Windy Mountain, especially after meeting Hort and Mudge and Carrick. But then, instead of that youth Mat, the Bragget villagers would have flogged him, an innocent stranger, had the dog Shadow not rescued him. He sighed. It seemed that for every Carrick and Hort and Mudge there was a host of people just waiting to come down on his head. Well, if a strange master was inevitable, he'd choose his own, to protect himself. "Which would be the best?" he said at last.

Harga shot him an old-fashioned look. "The best wizard, or the best teacher? Or the one you'd best like?"

Gom sighed heavily. "Tell me their names."

"Well now." Harga considered. "There's Tolasin. He's very learned. He's also kind, wise, and patient—as wizards go. In fact," Harga said, "he was my teacher." A smile tugged the corner of her mouth. "You'll not have to say who sent you."

He didn't answer her smile. "The others—they'd recognize me also?"

"Doubtless, unfortunately."

"What if they ask about you?"

"They shouldn't. It isn't done. But if they do, just say I've gone away."

"Tolasin—how do I find him?"

Harga took an oatcake, spread on raspberry jam. "You don't. He'll find you." She set down her knife. "I couldn't reach him last night. But I'll try again today, and keep trying. If I succeed by the time I go, I'll leave him word about you. You, meanwhile, will hold tight and wait."

"Wait—where?"

"In Pen'langoth, in your Jolly Fisherman. You see, if he's not in time, that's where you put word out for one of the others."

"The Jolly Fisherman? That's an odd place to seek a wizard."

"As a matter of fact," Harga said, "that's the most likely place to find one right now, if few guess it."

"Why is that?"

"You've heard of Perelion the Wanderer?"

"No-o." Who was he? Another wizard, or tinker, perhaps?

"Perelion is an errant furnace, a wandering star."

A *wandering* star? "Not one of the Realms, then?"

"No, Gom. That bright string lies below our horizon, anyway. Over the Southern Oceans. No, Perelion is something else again."

Gom glanced to the windows. He knew the northern twins that Hort and Carrick had taught him take direction from, but they stayed fixed. "I don't know it, Mother."

"Not surprising, for it passes this way only every seven years." Harga pointed upward. "For the past two months, Perelion has been climbing from the southern horizon until now it's overhead. If you hadn't had so much on your mind these past weeks, you'd have noticed it. Very soon, twenty-six nights' hence, in fact, it will pass between the twins. During that time their combined light will be such that they'll seem to form one great brilliant star, brighter than the full moon, even. This conjunction, which we call Unity, lasts fourteen nights. Unity is considered by wizards a most auspicious time. On the first night, they gather secretly in Pen'langoth for the Great Covenance. They deal with outstanding Council matters, review members' rankings—and give their apprentices Final Examinations in sorcery. Then, as Perelion breaks free and goes its way, the wizards wind up their business, collect new assistants, and go home—for another seven years."

Seven years! "It takes *seven years* to qualify?" He'd certainly make his own choice!

"To *train:* there's no guarantee of qualification."

Gom's chin came up.

"I'm not suggesting you won't make the grade on your own account. But while wizards like to have someone to grub for them; to fetch and to carry, the fact is that Ulm is small, and the Hierarchy guards its numbers jealously.

They fail as many as they can. Often as few as one will
graduate, but mostly, none at all. Yet still young hopefuls
come knocking on their door at Unity."

"Huh," Gom said. That didn't sound very fair. "Will
Tolasin be at the Covenance?"

"I think not." Harga smiled. "He doesn't go to meet-
ings anymore. Hasn't taken an apprentice in a while,
either, so I heard. I'm hoping he'll take you, for my sake.
But if not—then you must seek your master the regular
way, which is why you must go to Pen'langoth in any
case, and why I shall ask Tolasin to meet you there—a
great concession, that will be."

Gom nodded. He could well imagine, wizards being
such important people. Two or three wizards, Harga had
said. "If Tolasin somehow doesn't work out, I'm to seek
one of the others, is that it?" But the Covenance lasted
only fourteen days. What if Tolasin didn't show up early?
What then? He wouldn't want to miss his next choice.
"How do I judge how long to wait, Mother?"

"Ah, that's the trick. You'll need a lot of luck and
common sense—but then you're blessed with both."

Gom's cheeks grew warm at the compliment. He rushed
to prove his worth. "You said Unity, and the Covenance,
was only twenty-six nights away. Shall I get to Pen'langoth
in time?" On Carrick's map, the lakes looked quite far
from the Dunderfosse.

"I hope so—with Stormfleet's help."

Gom blew out his cheeks. "Sounds simple enough
then. Who are the other two wizards?"

"The first is Folgan." Harga looked wry. "He's a hard
man—even harsh at times, especially with fools—by
fools he means apprentices."

"If he's that awful, why give me his name?"

Harga smiled. "He's brilliant in all the fields of necromancy. And he's a very important man, second only to Mecrim Thurgeril, the Grand Archimage himself."

"Grand Archimage?"

"The head of the Council, the highest wizard in all Ulm."

"But—isn't that you?"

Harga laughed shortly. "I'm a bit of a maverick, Gom," she said. "And outside the Hierarchy. Failing Tolasin, Folgan is your next choice."

Gom thought otherwise. "How do I find him?"

"Very simply, by putting out the right word in the right place. Each wizard has a pass phrase. Folgan's is *the crow flies north.*"

"The crow flies north," Gom repeated. "Where do I say it?" he asked, and guessed, even as he spoke. "In The Jolly Fisherman! How?"

"You must sit in the parlor of an evening, and say the phrase, it doesn't matter when."

Gom looked dubious, remembering Essie's noisy parlor. "How loudly?"

"Just in your normal voice. It will be heard."

"What then?"

"Then you wait. Someone will be sitting there—you'll never spot who it is. That messenger will take your invocation to Folgan. Within the next day or two, you'll know whether he'll see you or not."

"Not? Oh. He might already have his new apprentice."

"Or he might simply refuse Harga's son. He and I are not on good terms."

Gom breathed in secret relief. "Why not?"

Harga cocked her eye. "As I said, I'm a maverick. But much as he dislikes me," she went on seriously, "he's a just man, and it's more than likely he'll take you on your merit."

Hmm. But Gom wouldn't take him. "Who's the other?"

"Bokar Riffik. A good man, not as clever as Folgan, and lacking an original mind. Also, he tends to the soft side, so his apprentices don't thrive in their final tests, and even if they pass, they never amount to much."

"Then why give me his name?"

"First, Bokar lives close to the lakelands, and he specializes in dealing with people—which would be good for you. And second, you would not, as his other apprentices have done, be inclined to laziness, lacking the goad. You have the will to learn, your own inner drive."

Gom flushed at the praise. "I find him the same way?"

Harga nodded. "His invocation is *the winds of change are blowing*."

"The winds of change are blowing," Gom repeated bleakly. Cold winds, stripping away the last shreds of his old familiar world. Soon he'd be alone—no Harga, no rune, with only three names to hang on to.

Harga gathered up the dishes. "Courage. You'll succeed, I know it. My worry is Stormfleet. Whether he'll carry you to Pen'langoth."

"Oh," Gom said quickly. "He will, all right. He's my friend."

"Maybe. But should he, is what I'm wondering, and whether we ought even to ask him."

"Oh, I see," Gom said, disgusted at his thoughtlessness. The moment the priceless cito set foot out of the Dunderfosse, folk on every hand would hunt him down. And Gom had been so rapt in his own problems, he'd forgotten about Stormfleet's. "I suppose he should stay here."

Harga nodded. "I'll offer him refuge, of course," she said. "But I can't see that one putting out to graze with a nanny goat while you go careening about the countryside alone. As for me, I'm in two minds. He should stay here, but then how will you get to Pen'langoth in time for the Covenance?" She beckoned Gom over to the sink. "Let's get rid of these dishes," she said. "Then go see what Stormfleet has to say."

They found the cito on the shore beyond the holly screen, looking out across the lake. His very stance, the toss of his head when he saw them told Gom that already he chafed to be off.

Gom turned uncertainly to Harga, waiting for her to speak, but she merely gestured him on.

"Harga has to go away," Gom said bluntly, amazed at how matter-of-fact he sounded. "And I'm leaving here first thing tomorrow."

"Good." Stormfleet whinnied with pleasure. "It's time to move on, though I've enjoyed my stay," he added to Harga. "Where to next?"

"I have to go to Pen'langoth to find myself a master. There isn't much time, so I'd be glad if you'd take me there. Though I warn you, perhaps you should stay here."

Stormfleet tossed his head proudly. "Stay here? I'm a horse, not a mouse! Of course I'll take you, and never mind the danger."

"But you should mind." Harga spoke now. "You run great risk going to Pen'langoth."

"I was not born to be put out to pasture," neighed Stormfleet. "Besides, Gom has need of me."

"Mmmm," Harga said. "I understand you're promised to Urolf, the Yul Kinta lord."

"Aye, as all us citos are promised to that folk."

"Why?" Gom asked. "Why is that?"

"Because the Yul Kinta, like Stormfleet, are well nigh immortal."

Immortal. Gom's eyes gleamed. "What do they look like?"

A quick smile lit Harga's face. "Human enough, just as Stormfleet looks like a regular horse. But don't let that fool you. They're a different race entirely. They walked the forests of Ulm long before man rose from the primordial slime. Their powers are great, and quite different from mine. They see things the ordinary man cannot, their gift of prophecy is legendary, and beware of any who can look into your heart."

"Do men know of them?" Carrick hadn't mentioned them, as far as Gom could recall.

"They know of them, may even have seen them the rare times that secret folk have left their forests openly for the public domain."

"Are there many?"

"There once wasn't a woodland of any consequence as didn't hold an enclave. But now there are few. They've ever been, and remain a fierce folk, quick to take offense, and territorially inclined." She looked to Stormfleet, back to Gom again. "Lord Urolf's enclave lives not far south of the Dunderfosse."

"So close!" Gom laid his hand on Stormfleet's back protectively.

"Urolf will be looking for you, friend," Harga told the cito, "to right what he must see as grave wrong, and restore his honor."

Stormfleet pawed the ground and flared his nostrils. "Let him look. All he'll find is a clean pair of heels!"

"I would hope so for your sake, Stormfleet." Harga turned to Gom. "You also. Urolf will hunt you too, to settle the score. If you'd not spend your majority behind bars, watch out." She switched back to Stormfleet. "I repeat, you'd do well to consider staying here," she said, "unless . . ." She broke off, gazing across the water.

Fine thing, Gom thought glumly. How was he ever going to reach Pen'langoth in time? Not on Stormfleet, not after all this talk, for he'd not let the cito put himself at such risk, whatever was said.

Harga turned back. "Stormfleet, there is one way you could go about Ulm without danger or harm, now and for the rest of your life," she said slowly.

Gom's face brightened. A magic gift for Stormfleet? Of invisibility, perhaps? He pictured himself astride the cito's back, seemingly galloping along in midair. No, Harga wouldn't do a thing like that, for an invisible horse would attract as much attention as a cito.

"Say what it is," Stormfleet said.

"Urolf seeks a black colt with the cito ringmark on his brow. What if colt turned into, say, an old gray nag, lame, a bit knock-kneed, perhaps?"

Gom's eyes shone. He'd guessed right. "You mean, you'd put a sort of spell on him, so that people won't see him as he really is?"

"Not exactly. The change would be real."

Gom sucked in his breath. "No!"

Harga turned back to Stormfleet. "Though if you could sham the limp and knock-knees, I could spare you the worst, and leave you fairly fit and fine. What do you say?"

"A minute." Stormfleet turned about and trotted off along the beach. Gom made to follow, but Harga held him. "It's his decision," she murmured. "Let him be."

They waited. Gom gazed at his friend, at the sun's sheen on the glossy back, the long, wiry mane lifting in the wind, the grace of his stance as he stood staring out over the water to the farther shore. Gom couldn't bear to think of Stormfleet looking less than he did then.

Presently, the cito came back, halted before them.

"I'll do it," he said.

Chapter Seven

"NO!" GOM CRIED. "I won't let you!"

"Don't get so heated," Stormfleet said. "It won't be forever. Just until you can change me back again."

"Wait," Harga said. "Gom can make no such promise."

Stormfleet tossed his head and shook out his mane. "Did I ask for one? But I trust when he's as you, he'll know how to do it."

"You trust too much," Harga said. "The reversing spell is difficult, and the outcome uncertain even in the best of circumstances."

"Hrrmph." Stormfleet looked away. "I'll risk it, even so."

"Good." Harga patted the cito's neck, turned to go. "I'll make the potion." She moved off back to the house.

Stormfleet pushed Gom gently with his nose. "Go. Help your dam."

"But you—" Gom stopped. The cito's voice brooked no argument. Gom took off after Harga, caught her by the arm. "The spell *is* reversible?"

"Aye—in principle." Harga pulled free.

"What do you mean?"

"As I said, it's not an easy one." She made to move on.

"Then there's no guarantee. And it could be years, *years,* before we'd have a chance to put it to the test."

He blocked her path. "What," he demanded fiercely, "if I don't become a wizard? What then?"

"Nay, in that case, Stormfleet would be the least of our worries," she said, pushing past him. "Listen, your friend knows full well the risk, is ready to take it. His wish, not yours, is at issue here."

"He's a horse, Mother. A *horse!*"

Harga turned on him. "That makes him less fit to choose than you? It seems to me, son, that horse or no, your cito lacks neither the ability to weigh his choices —nor the courage to act upon them!"

"And what does that mean!" Gom called after her, but Harga had gone in.

In silence, Gom helped Harga light the stove, assemble all the right tools and ingredients. All his life he'd longed for this, and now? His jaw clamped tight. He remembered Stormfleet in the solahinn's moonlit pen, the beautiful and terrible dark form rearing over him, threatening to bring its hooves crashing down onto his head. Not fair, not fair, that the most wondrous horse in the world was to be changed into a decrepit nag!

"Do you have to make him so old and ugly!" he demanded suddenly. "Why not just different—a roan, or a piebald, or something?"

Harga's eyes flashed. "Don't you think I would if I could? But that's a far more subtle magic, and there just isn't time!" She gave him a dish to hold while she poured potions into it, and stirred them together until the mixture began to smoke. The brew's stink brought hot bile into Gom's throat. His breakfast churning, he turned his face away.

"It's tipping, Gom," Harga said sharply.

He righted the dish, his anger rekindling. "You don't look one bit sorry."

"I can't afford to. If I don't concentrate, the mixture will mutate, and goodness knows what will happen when Stormfleet drinks it."

"Drinks!" Gom stared down in horror.

"You expect it to taste like honey, considering its aim?" Harga snapped. "You can go back down now, if you like. I'll finish alone."

"No," Gom said lamely. "I'll stay."

"Good." She took the bowl from him. "You see that bottle by your left elbow? Pull its stopper and pass it— and be quick!"

Harga set the mixture aside to ferment. "He must take it tonight," she said. "By early starlight."

She went to the crystal globe still on the table by the stove and cupped her hands about it, murmuring. Gom moved up behind her, watching, listening intently, trying vainly to catch her words. At last, she straightened up.

"Tolasin's still not there."

"May I see?"

She moved aside.

It was now, Gom saw, like looking into a fragile bubble. Within its bright depths bulged a stone chamber: jumble of boxes, books, and bottles. Tolasin's workshop —but no Tolasin.

"Never mind," Harga said. "I'll keep trying."

She made Gom a bath before the kitchen hearth, laying out clean pants that tied with a cord, and tunic of coarse cotton. "My sleeping suit, Gom," she said. "Not exactly what you might wear about Pen'langoth, but 'twill do until I've fixed your poor clothes. Give them here."

Gom undressed, turned out his pockets, setting his treasures carefully on the kitchen table: the coins Carrick had given him to spend in Pen'langoth market, the little wooden box of tiny loder seeds, a gold flake, memento of his find under Windy Mountain.

Harga picked up the box, turned it about. "That's a piece of fine carving, Gom. Did your father make it?"

"No. I did," Gom said proudly. "The first good thing I ever made, Father said. Look inside."

Harga raised the lid, shook the tiny loder seeds lightly. "What treasure," she said. "To think, you carry in your pocket the makings of a forest!" Setting the box down again, she took up the flake, and held it to the light. "Ah, yes: the gold. Mandrik did his part right well." She smiled. "And so did you, Gom, as I knew you would. Give me this flake, and I'll put it to good use."

Gom nodded. For years he'd carried that bright token scored by Skeller's broad, flat thumbnail. Now at last, he thought in a rush of warm feeling, he could do something to please Harga, and make up for his outburst. "It's yours, Mother. Take it."

After his bath, they had elevenses, then Harga sent Gom down to Stormfleet. "I'll come soon," she said. "But there are one or two things I have to do first."

A couple of hours later, she joined them by the orchard, and sat, her sewing basket open beside her, and began to mend his clean dry breeches and the oversized shirt that Carrick had lent him.

Gom lay back, gazing up into the blue sky, thinking

of the stars invisible in the sun's bright fire: the fixed northern twins, Perelion the Wanderer; the Seven Realms of the Heavens, bright necklace strung across the skies below the southern horizon. It still seemed strange to Gom that those tiny points of light should be big and hot as the sun, or whole worlds like Ulm, only bigger. What did Ulm look like from those distant worlds? Too small for notice, probably. He snorted. Blob of dirt, indeed! He thought of the shining crystal stair, and the sky hall, and the wondrous crystal pillar, the Tamarith, star-gate that Jastra had set above the High Vargue before Faramor, Yul Kinta, or human walked the world. "How old is Jastra, Mother?"

Her needle paused. "So it finally occurred to you." Her fingers moved on. "I don't know. You see, time is different among the stars. For every day that passes up there, years go by down here, so Jastra says. I still can't see it quite."

Gom sat up, stricken. "And you're going— When you come back, I'll be old—dead, even!"

"No!" She held up her rune. "This holds my immortality sign. From the moment of your birth it has worked its power even into your bones. That power will hold forever, without the rune. You'll live as long as Stormfleet—barring accidents—and live long you must!"

Gom stayed motionless, in the thrall of Harga's words. Immortality sign? He glanced to where Stormfleet stood grazing. He'd live as long as his friend! He let out a slow, quiet breath, remembering: . . . *and under the rune's enchantment, the child shall grow slowly and slowly, like heart of oak, not counting the years as others* . . . Now he understood why he'd not grown older as his brothers and sisters had, why Stig had aged and died while Harga had remained the same. *Immortality.* Another gift of Harga. Of course, the gift had come with a price. "Your long-lived tool," he murmured, but he was smiling. It didn't matter. She loved him, she'd said it, loved him more than she'd dreamed she would. He lay back down again and closed his eyes.

"Is Jastra more powerful than you?"

"What makes you say that?"

Gom turned his head and looked at her. "He sent you from the stair. And we don't have anything like that stair, and that sky hall, and the Tamarith."

Harga looked up from her sewing. "I let myself be sent. I trust Jastra. We haven't those things as you say, nor have we spread among the stars." She set the sewing down on her lap and fixed Gom squarely with her eye. "So I admit they do seem a more powerful folk than we. But—"

Gom came up again.

"—to make magic, Gom, really great magic, you need knowledge, and the power of mind and will. A great wizard collects many tools, and develops the strength to wield them. The Spinrathe, having the Tamarith crystal, have come to rely on it alone, neglecting other tools, and the schooling of their minds.

"This used not to be. When they first left Bayon for the other Realms, they crossed the heavens in shining ships. But once they learned to use the Tamariths as stargates, they let those ships rot, and lost their magic lore. On their worlds, Jastra tells me, they have the same means for making magic as we do. But they don't know how to use them. Without the Tree of Life, they have no magic, no power. Conversely, if Karlvod gets control of the Tamarith-awr-Bayon, he'll wield power absolutely."

Gom nodded slowly. He was beginning to see more clearly the threat of Karlvod. And that Harga, through her strength of will and versatility, was likely not only as powerful as Jastra, or Karlvod, but even more so. And that her magic might well prevail eventually against Karlvod and the Spohr. Katak had come to work Karlvod's will. But hadn't Harga's rune broken Katak's seal-spell and shut him in his own trap? The desire surged within Gom to be on his way, to start along his wizard's path, so that he and Harga could stand together against Lord Karlvod and the Spohr. Meanwhile, as she had said, they must each take their separate ways. "You will take care, Mother, won't you?"

She took up her sewing again. "I'll try, Gom. I'll try."

As the day drew to a close, Harga shook out her finished mending, folded it, and stood. "You can see Perelion now," she said, pointing skyward.

Gom climbed to his feet, and followed her direction. The Wanderer, no longer overhead, had moved closer to the northern twins. The moving star certainly made those around it seem small and dim by comparison. "It has a faint violet color," he said. "It looks very mysterious." The twins drew his eye, two more bright spots, growing brighter by the minute in the deepening sky. Gom pointed. "Do they have names, too?"

"Aye. The left-hand star is called Frydd. The right, Munyr."

"Frydd, Munyr," Gom repeated. "They sound like people." All three stars, the twins and Perelion, formed a long, narrow triangle in the sky, like a sliver of cake, a sliver that would grow shorter and shorter for the next twenty-six nights, so Harga said, until it condensed at last to a single brilliant point of light. Gom could see quite clearly the path that Perelion would take to reach the twins, the space between the two stars where the Wanderer would pass during the fourteen nights of Unity.

"Strange," Gom murmured, his eye still fixed on the trio. "Perelion moves fast to reach the twins in only twenty-six nights. And yet it will stay by them for a whole fourteen days thereafter."

Harga looked pleased. "That is only one of the mysteries of that star. There are many legends explaining it. One is that Frydd and Munyr are twin sisters. Perelion, born wanderer, in love with each equally, cannot choose either one over the other. Every seven years, his mind made up at last, he races toward them. The moment he sees them, he's again confused, and so he lingers, unable to choose, unable to break free. So great is his effort to make a choice, the legend goes, its influence drifts down and permeates the whole world. So if any choice is to be made, any path taken, it should be by Perelion's light, during Unity." Harga turned to Stormfleet. "Are you still inclined, friend?"

"Aye."

She went into the house, taking Gom's mended clothes and the sewing gear with her. Gom laid his head on Stormfleet's flank, stroked the shiny coat.

"Don't look so downcast," the cito said. "It won't be forever."

Gom stepped back. "How can you be so brave!"

"Stupid, is what you're really thinking." Stormfleet

swished his tail. "I'm neither brave, nor stupid. I know, I might not get changed back again, but if I'm to live a halfway decent life, that chance I must take. I can only thank Harga for such an offer—but then, she's a wizard."

Gom turned away. He was beginning to see there was more to sorcery than knowing mixtures and such. One also needed the wisdom and courage to apply them. Having struck the bargain with Stormfleet, she'd made the potion early, giving the cito plenty of time to reconsider. And she hadn't been too squeamish to make it, either. Gom hung his head. Presumptuous fool, to have judged his mother so. To have judged her at all!

The sky was almost dark when Harga held the bowl under Stormfleet's nose.

"Whrrrrrrr-brrrrrr!" The cito involuntarily shied away. Then, snorting, he dunked his nose and drained the bowl. When he'd done, he raised his head, his muzzle dripping. "I don't feel different."

"You won't, not yet. The change will come slowly by starlight whilst you sleep," Harga said. "And you'll not endure it alone. Gom and I shall come and keep you company through the night, brave friend, but first, he and I have business between us."

Chapter Eight

THEY ATE a simple supper. When they had done, Harga held out her hand. "Let's take a look at your peddler's map."

Gom spread Carrick's parchment on the table, and they bent their heads together under the lamplight. Harga laid her finger on a river that flowed south from the Dunderfosse. "This is where you'll come out—don't worry, the forest will steer you, just as it steered you the short distance to me. It's about six days to the southern border. From there, follow the river to the hills, then go southeast until you come to these." She tapped a ring of barrier hills north of Sundor. "But on no account cross them."

From those hills, Harga went on, they would go directly east, and fast, across the Wilds, a perilous tract, his mother said, that no sane man ever crossed alone. She drew her finger across the center of the map, coming at last to the nub end of the mountain range that formed the western side of Long Valley. "You'll go around the Sidliths, passing under the walls of Hornholm, and Medgan, and Dune." She tapped the names dotted about the foothills. "Past them, you'll out come onto a main trading road, and reach Pen'langoth well within your twenty-six days."

Gom eyed the route that Harga had just drawn. "Seems clear, Mother."

Harga folded up the map, handed it back. "Aye, as most plans do. But they have a habit of taking their own shape, so be prepared for anything. Keep out of Sundor, race across the Wilds, and watch for Yul Kinta at all times, even though they're west of where you're going."

She took Gom up to the darkened chamber above, where once more she looked into the globe, but still no luck. To Gom's disgust, she made him repeat all that he had to do when he got to Pen'langoth. "Go to The Jolly Fisherman," he counted off on his fingers. "Wait to hear from Tolasin, and—"

"I've been thinking, Gom," Harga said. "You can't afford to wait too long, or you'll likely miss out altogether. If he doesn't show up seven days into Unity, then put out your first pass phrase."

Gom bristled. After saying he had enough common sense to make his own choices, Harga was now making them for him!

"Folgan's next," she reminded him.

Gom looked away.

"Now," Harga said briskly. "Make a wish."

A wish? Gom stared in surprise. A wish! His only wish was one Harga couldn't possibly fulfill: that she dismiss last night's events as a false vision and go on as before. A wish. Gom sat down in his armchair, rested his chin in his hands. He wished to become a wizard, which only he could bring about, so Harga said. To live until Harga came back. The immortality sign had taken care of this. To restore the cito's true form someday. Harga had already said there was no guarantee of that. So what else? He hunched forward in his chair, lost in thought. Finally, he sat up. "I wish," he said, "that I might have my teacher this year."

"I cannot grant a wish like that in such a rush," she said. "Nor would it be wise even if I could. Wish again, for something more modest, and that you yourself can help along."

"I wish . . . for a spell to help me find my teacher."

Harga nodded. "That I can grant." She drew him to a bench by the wall, under clustered windows through which high Perelion shone. On the bench a smooth black stone about the shape and size of an oatcake gleamed in the starlight. Harga took Gom's left hand, placed it over the stone. Then, taking up a dark silken shawl, she shook it out, threw it over his head, and let it float down around him, enclosing him with the stone.

Through the flimsy stuff of the shawl, Gom saw Harga's slight shape haloed against the violet beams. He watched her turn to the windowed stars, and raise her arms, and he heard her chanting:

"Demerian, Valarian, and Quiorthar:
Thriorfan, Mastrogan, Phyllyriar!"

The stone flared under his hand, so bright that he saw his very finger bones outlined against its glare, and something swirled about that tiny space, not a wind, not anything he could put name to, but it scattered goosebumps up his arms. He closed his eyes, took a deep breath, stayed silent.

His mother's quiet voice startled him. "Open your eyes, Gom."

He did so. The shawl still covered his head, his hand was still on the stone. How long had he been standing there? He tried to move, in vain. Only after Harga pulled away the shawl could he stir, and with great effort raise his numbed hand off the stone to chafe it back to life.

Harga shook the shawl, folded it, and set it aside. "The magic that I have laid about you should pull a mentor to you. But also heed this warning: it may not be the one you expect; neither," she reminded him again, "does the gaining guarantee your success. That must be of your own making."

Gom nodded. "I understand, Mother. Is the spell done?"

"Done. Now: take off your belt."

Gom unbuckled his belt, laid it on the table, then turned to find his mother holding out something neatly coiled in her hand.

He took it, unrolled it, letting it dangle. It was a brand-new brown leather belt with a beautifully stitched pouch embossed with sun, and moon, and stars—but his eye went straight to the shining silver buckle. He held the buckle to the lamp, the better to see. It was square, with two wide outer posts, a thinner one in the middle, like any other buckle, except that the right-hand post was shaped like a bear, and the left, a sparrow poised for flight. A wonderful belt. For him?

"Try it on, try it on," Harga said.

With shaking hands, Gom slipped the new belt around his middle, threaded it through the buckle, pulled it to fit. It was light, and soft, without the usual stiffness of new leather.

"Umm," Harga said, her head to one side. "Looks well. You like it?"

"I love it! Is—is it mine?"

"In exchange for this." Harga took up his discarded belt. "Agreed?"

Gom stared at the scuffed, worn, stained old thing in perplexity. "Why, yes," he said.

To his surprise, Harga fastened it around her middle with great care, then settled her blouse in place. "At least I'll have something of you with me. Now," she went on, "open your pouch."

Gom raised the pouch's flap, thrust his fingers inside and drew out a small crystal on a stout silver chain.

" 'Tis your new talisman, to make up for the rune."

He held the crystal to the light. In its rainbow depths something flickered, tiny yellow spangle catching Perelion's beams. He turned, his eyes wide. "My flake of gold!" Magically encased within the crystal shard. "How?" he cried. *"When* did you do that?"

She only smiled.

After elevenses, that was when, he thought. Before she came out to the orchard. "Is there—is there any enchantment in it?"

"Oh, yes." Harga gestured to her globe. "Remember how we went to see Jastra? Well that stone is imbued with the same magic power. I've worn it long. But—I do not need it now. If any time the stone should flash, close your hand about it, and you'll stand once more by the crystal stair. *Alamar.* If you should be asleep, or otherwise engaged, the gold flake will call you with a waking dream. Then, who knows, you and I may meet and talk awhile."

Gom slipped the crystal over his head, and let it dangle against his shirt. Felt comfortable. He closed his hand about it.

"I have one more gift for you, but that will wait until tomorrow. Let's go to Stormfleet. He needs our company this night."

As they carried their bedding outside, Stormfleet emerged silently from the orchard. Gom ran to him, and barely refrained from crying out. The coat was no longer sleek and shiny. The hair felt coarse and wiry and uneven under his hand. But he said nothing.

Harga spread her pallet, and turned to Stormfleet. "We're with you if you need us. As for me, tomorrow's going to be a long day, so I'll say good night." She lay down and pulled her blanket over her.

Fine company she is, Gom thought. He took up his bedding, slung it over his shoulder, followed Stormfleet over to the orchard. There, he spread his pad, sat down against an apple tree, resolved to sit the night out to its bitter end.

"Go to sleep," said Stormfleet. "Didn't you hear your dam?"

Gom hugged his knees. "I'm keeping watch."

"Then I'll wish you joy in it," Stormfleet snorted. "I myself shall take a nap. I am unaccountably tired."

Not unaccountably, thought Gom. He remembered how strange Harga's wishing spell had made him feel. The enchantment was working.

Wind wafted through the trees, gently lifting Stormfleet's mane, mingling cold drafts with air still warm from the sun.

Gom stayed upright, determined to watch all night,

despite Stormfleet's ingratitude. His hand went as of old to his chest, encountered the unfamiliar edges of the crystal. He drew it out, held it to the starlight, admiring its gleam. "See what Harga gave me," he said. But Stormfleet was fast asleep. Harga also. Gom let the crystal fall, hurt at being so deserted. Then finally Harga's intent broke upon him: no need to make a martyr of himself: just being here was enough. Gom slid down, turned on his side, and pulled his blanket over his head.

It was barely light when Gom felt himself being shaken gently awake. He sat up, dazed, to find Harga bent over him. "Hush, Gom. It is done. Keep you calm, and quiet, d'you hear? Here is your friend." She moved aside.

Gom stared. Oh, oh, oh! An old gray nag stood before him, watching him with hollowed, rheumy eyes. The noble brow was gone, and the shining silver ringmark. Gom looked down. The creature's knees looked swollen, and turned in. The sagging back with bony ribs that Gom could count was hung with dull gray hair, almost threadbare in patches.

"Well, do you have to stare?" Stormfleet snapped. "Have you never seen a horse before?"

Gom said not a word.

"You'll get used to it," the cito said, softening. "I admit it's harder for you than me, for I can't see myself."

"How do you feel?" Gom said.

"Fairly fine. I'll show you." Stormfleet led the way onto the beach. Gom followed sadly. The colt stood a full hand shorter, and his back sagged in the middle.

"Wait here." Stormfleet trotted to the end of the open

stretch, then, turning about, broke into a gallop the length of the shore.

Gom could hardly bear to watch. Stormfleet was not exactly a cripple. But his speed was gone, and his fiery grace. He turned on Harga. "He's not the same!"

"Who said he would be?" Harga answered. "But the price is not as high as it might have been. See," she said, as Stormfleet pulled up and trotted back to join them in some semblance of his old easy gait.

The cito whickered. "Remember, Mistress, what you said yesterday about the finch and the sparrow? Now we are three!" The cito led them back into the garden, walking like his old self, until suddenly, he pulled up short. "Ooops," he said. He drooped his head, turned in his feet until his knees knocked together, then with painful exaggeration limped off to graze.

Gom, unsmiling, followed Harga to breakfast. While she toasted cakes, he went to his room, changed back into his own cleaned and mended clothes. Then he sat on his bed as yet unslept in, gazed wryly around the pale blue sunlit chamber. Seven years, *seven years* before he'd finally sleep under the gaze of that wooden owl! He took up his staff and returned to the kitchen.

After breakfast, Harga made him a small pack for the journey. Gom watched her fill his water bottle, Stig's green glass bottle that she must have recognized. "You can have that, Mother!" he cried impulsively, then realized how much he would miss it.

She handed it over with a smile and a shake of her head. "Nay. I think you'd feel its loss too much."

Gom took it, relieved. And yet he couldn't get the

thought of her face out of his mind when she'd spoken of Stig. On a sudden idea, he took out his box of seeds. "Keep this, then, for Father and me."

Harga took it, her eyes brimming with tears. "Oh, Gom." She busied herself anew, fitting his pack with traveler's biscuits, apples, and fruit cake, then tied the pack to a bedroll. Gom walked downstairs a last time, and with Stormfleet followed Harga through the holly screen and onto the shore.

The raft journey was quiet.

Gom sat with his back to the island, not caring to see it recede. At the other side, Harga tied up the raft, and jumped ashore.

"Your other gift, Gom. Guard it well." She produced a plain silver ring, placed it on the fourth finger of his right hand. "Your key to the Dunderfosse, and to this island. If you would come home, come to the edge of the forest, turn the ring three times following the path of the sun, and the ways will open to you, bringing you to this place. But when you reach this spot, this is what you'll see." Harga turned to the lake, and waved her arm once. Lake and island vanished, replaced by a valley floor. Astonished, Gom bent, felt about. The ground seemed real enough. He walked out a little way, where water should be, found grass underfoot.

"How—" he began.

Harga laid a finger across her lips. "Turn the ring thrice sunwise and the lake will reappear. Try it now— but come back here to me first!"

Gom returned to Harga's side, and twirled his ring three times from east to west. Immediately, lake and cliff reappeared! Gom gazed about in awe. "If only we could have done this with Stormfleet," he said.

"You think I would not if there had been time?"

Gom hung his head. Harga had told him how difficult the process was.

"Come home, Gom, when you need, for as long as you need, only mind when you leave to "lock up" by turning your ring countersunwise."

"And when I leave the forest also?"

Harga shot him a smile. "No need. Just say where you would come out, and the ways will steer you. Then close behind you—snap shut, I should say, when you step from these borders." Now she was solemn again. "I can't say when we'll meet again, my dear. Only know that this is your home—workshop, and all in it. Study my books, my chronicles with care, but be sure before you would use any magic that you know how to work it well first— and keep things orderly against my return.

"Gom—I wish there had been time. Mayhap, one day—" Her voice trailed off. Then she rallied. "Until then, my blessing and great good wishes go with you, and with you, noble friend, and may you both get your heart's desire." She put her arms around Gom and hugged him hard.

At last they broke apart, and Harga stepped onto the raft. "Again: the forest will put you where you need to go. Only beware of the Yul Kinta," she said. She picked up the paddle, and turned. "Good-bye, Gom. Remember you're of the sparrow and the bear!"

Choked, Gom could only watch Harga push off from the shore, move smoothly out onto the water. Wind caught his mother's skirts, billowed them out like a sail, teased a wisp of hair from the coil at her nape. He watched the tiny figure paddling under the lee of the cliff, and still stood as, reaching the corner, she gave one last wave, and disappeared.

Chapter Nine

THEY DESCENDED in silence onto the forest floor, Gom, digging his staff into the soft moist loam, retracing in his mind the joyous journey of only two days before, when he and Harga and the great and glorious cito colt had tramped triumphantly up the ridge to Harga's lake.

If only he'd known they'd part again so soon. Gom sighed. It wouldn't have made any difference. Even after he had known, he'd been at odds with her, over Storm-fleet, and this and that.

What was Harga doing now? Getting ready for her journey? How would she reach the crystal stair? He hadn't asked, neither had she thought fit to tell him. He pictured her there, climbing the crystal stair to the sky hall, to the tree that was no tree but a crystal pillar. Tamarith. *Star-gate.* He thought of the light shafting down from its heights. The shimmering shape of Jastra slowly forming until it looked quite solid and real. Not Jastra in person, but only his image: alamar-Jastra, locked in the bright beam. And yet—Gom would bet that was how the real Jastra came. If so, then Harga would leave by the same way. He trudged along blindly, intent. He pictured her going to the tree, through the unseen barrier that had kept Gom from it. He saw her waiting beside it for the bright, enveloping beam. And then? Would she feel a whirlwind, as he'd felt when the rune's magic had lifted him from the High Vargue and set him in the middle of the Dunderfosse, close by Harga's secret domain? Or the shimmering he'd felt, going alamar with Harga to the crystal stair? He pictured her racing past the stars, as even now Perelion the Wanderer arced over Ulm's skies.

He recalled her bending over the hearth, dark eyes reflecting the warmth of the flames; going up the lamplit stair to her workshop; lying in her armchair, face cold and stiff; buckling on his old belt with care; her last words to him: *Remember you're of the sparrow and the bear.*

Gom and Stormfleet pushed on through soft, thick undergrowth. As Harga had promised, the path ever opened before them, and closed in their wake, leaving no trace of their passing. Enchanted forest, enchanted lake; a strange and wonderful house; the most remarkable mother in all Ulm: lost, because of the Spinrathe: Lord Karlvod and his deadly Spohr; Jastra and his doomsday gate.

Six days it should take them, Harga had said, to reach the forest edge.

Gom tried to think beyond to Tolasin and Pen'langoth, but ever his mind bent back to Harga. After but two days, *two days,* they were taking their separate paths. Harga up the crystal stair, and he—well, was he not also setting his feet upon one, in a way? One that would test his nerve and will? Wouldn't his climb, no less than the crystal stair, or the sacrificial bridge of the Onder, also demand hardship and self-sacrifice? Just as by climbing the stair Harga was leaving behind son, home, and world, so was Gom in taking his own appointed way losing mother, home, and world, in a way. Gom squared his shoulders, and quickened his pace. Like Harga, he would cheerfully do his part, climb his own crystal stair. *Remember you're of the sparrow and the bear . . .* Harga believed in him, and rightly so: hadn't he overcome Karlvod's Spohr, and taken her the rune? He'd have his master, Harga had as good as guaranteed it. So, his mouth curved at last into a smile: how could he fail?

For five days more they traveled the forest's slow paths, finding when they needed ripe fruits and seeds, good grass for Stormfleet, and fresh clear water to drink. Still thinking of Harga, Gom spoke little, and Stormfleet let him be. Then, sometime during the fifth day, Gom began to think ahead to Pen'langoth: the fishing quarter, the inn, the noisy marketplace. He swung his staff lightly, and, thrusting his free hand deep into his pocket, jingled Carrick's coins. What, he wondered, smiling at the thought of seeing the tinker again, had Carrick made of Gom's sudden disappearance? Moments after the man had sent him to buy himself some favor in the market, Gom had seen Zamul's face in the crowd. In a panic, he had fled back to the inn, and gotten himself trapped in a solahinn wagon moving east over the High Vargue.

Had the tavern folk told how he'd fled down the stair pursued by the man in bright green breeches? Essie the landlady, who'd been serving lunch in the parlor at the time, would surely have heard it from her chambermaids.

Gom wondered proudly what Shadow would make of the magnificent cito. Then, sighing, realized what the hound would really see. Oh, well. He didn't care what

Shadow thought anyway. To think he'd been hurt when Shadow chose Carrick for master over Gom as friend. Hah! Carrick could keep him, and good luck to them both.

By afternoon, the tree-gloom lightened, and tiny golden flashes of sun shot through the high leaves overhead. All at once, Gom heard the sound of running water. A little river gushed through the ferns to the right, and bending to the path, raced on. The air brightened, and they were through, gazing out across open land.

They stopped just inside the forest. The river flowed on, toward wooded hills on the skyline, where Harga had said they must go with all speed. Gom glanced south-westward, over the river, to where, Harga had warned him, lay Urolf's woodland seat.

Gom pointed his staff. "Can we make those hills by dusk?"

Stormfleet pawed the ground indignantly. "Don't be insulting!"

Looking back into the gloomy forest, Gom pictured the island hidden in its depths, the lake and house locked in Harga's enchantment; Jilly, her milk dried up, her discomfort over, grazing peacefully by the barn-cum-dairy. When he and Stormfleet stepped from the forest, it would close behind them, *snap shut,* Harga had said, half-jesting. He fingered his silver ring, key to his return. "Thank you for your hospitality," he called into the high branches. "Until I come again, farewell."

The trees waved in response, filling the air with a dry rustling sound, as Gom led Stormfleet into the open. The forest green closed after them, branches interlocking into a solid, impenetrable screen, so that now one could scarcely see where river emerged.

Gom slung staff and pack at his back, climbed astride Stormfleet—with ease, he sadly discovered. He recalled, as he felt the knobbles on that sagging spine, how he had clung precariously to the cito's high, broad, slippery back in the stampede from the solahinn stockade. "You're sure you don't feel as bad as you look, Stormfleet?"

Stormfleet arched his neck around, and bared his teeth. "One word more and I'll throw you!" The cito broke into a stiff gallop along the riverbank, a gait so unforgiving that Gom had to lie along his neck, clutching tightly to the stringy mane.

They reached the first trees just as the sun was setting.

Gom bathed in the river, and ate a light supper from his pack. As he ate, he eyed the grazing cito speculatively. "When we get to Pen'langoth," he said, "what shall I call you? And how explain you?"

"That's your problem." Stormfleet flicked his tail. "Choose any name that comes to mind. For the rest, I'm just a derelict you picked up along the way." He turned his head, a bunch of grass sticking out of his mouth, with such a mournful expression in his aged, sunken face that for the first time Gom could not forbear to laugh.

They left the river, and for three days traveled southeastward, just as Harga had said, up hill and down dale quick with creek and cascade. The woodland became denser, and smothered in wayfaring tree, or hobble bush, untidy tangles stretching from stand to rival stand of beech and wicopy.

Gom missed Harga sorely. At first, he wore her crystal inside his shirt, as he'd worn the rune, but after a while, he wore it out, for never know, he told himself, but that any moment it might flash, and alamar he'd climb the crystal stair, where her image would be waiting in the Tamarith's beam for a quick exchange. And as he lay down to sleep under the trees and wheeling stars, while Stormfleet moved quietly near, Gom would twist the unfamiliar ring around his finger, remembering how Harga had placed it there. His key to the Dunderfosse and his wondrous home and all Harga's marvelous treasure. Seven years: would he ever get to see it in all that time?

Perelion moved ever closer to the northerly twins. Seventeen more days to Unity, Gom reckoned one night, as they halted. By the map, they still had far to go. And while Harga had said they should get to Pen'langoth easily—she had also warned that plans often had a way of taking their own direction. Gom looked about warily. A dangerous time of day for small creatures, Acorn the squirrel had once warned him, not that Gom had needed telling. Beware of Yul Kinta, Harga had warned, even though you go east of their enclave. As Stormfleet wandered off to find grazing, Gom stood uncertain. He unslung his staff, but not his pack. And almost without thinking, slipped his crystal out of sight. Why did he feel so uneasy? Gom looked to Stormfleet, but he was off among the trees, head down unconcernedly.

A moment later, there came a quiet rustling in the trees ahead. A squirrel, perhaps? Or an early raccoon impatient to be out? The woods were alive with them. The rustling came again. Still no alert from Stormfleet. Even so. Gripping his staff tightly, Gom inched forward, dodging around tree trunks . . . and saw nothing. He reached a small clearing. Empty.

Relieved, he turned to go back—and found himself face to face with a man. Of middling height, and build, the stranger wore a mantle mottled in green, and brown, and gray. A hood hid the hair and shrouded the face in shadow. But though Gom could not see clearly, he'd swear that as he spun to face the man, there had come from under that hood a swift, quiet whisper of indrawn breath.

His eye fixed on the stranger, Gom heard Stormfleet move up behind him.

"Hey—who's he? And where did he come from so quick and quiet?"

Gom raised his staff. "Who are you?"

The man stepped closer, dipped his head politely. "I might ask the same of you, young sir," he said. The voice, neither deep nor high, and with a trace of accent, was mild enough.

Gom lowered his staff, some. His instinct told that this was no enemy. Even so. "I asked first," he said stubbornly.

The man bowed from the waist. "I am Feyrwarl, traveler, bound for Pen'langoth," he said, and doffed his hood. His brow was wide, his nose straight and long. His mouth was wide and deeply creased about as though he smiled a lot. The shock of thick black curls that fell to his shoulders was bound by a leather brow band.

Gom let out a deep breath. There was a certain air about the stranger that reminded him of Carrick. "Gom," he said, bowing awkwardly in return. "Gom Gobblechuck, of—"

Stormfleet whinnied alarm, cutting him off. "Don't be so hasty!"

Feyrwarl looked past Gom in disbelief. "That's yours?"
Gom glanced over his shoulder to where the cito hung
back in the bushes. "Withershins?" he said, thinking
quickly. "Not really. We, er, met along the road."

"I see," Feyrwarl said, then went on, a note of urgency
creeping into his voice, "Gom Gobblechuck, do you not
know that hereabouts isn't safe for chance strangers? That
not too far west of here live Yul Kinta?"

"I do," Gom said, uneasy again.

"Then move on with all speed, now," Feyrwarl urged.
"Where do you go?"

Gom saw no harm in that. "To the lakelands also,"
he conceded.

"I see. Take care that you not—" Feyrwarl stared out
into the darkness. "Too late, I'm afraid," he murmured.

Shrouded figures stepped from the trees, surrounding
Gom. Stormfleet neighed loudly.

Even as Gom heard the cito's warning, Feyrwarl turned.
"Pray meet Master Gom Gobblechuck, wayfarer," he said.

One of the figures, taller than Feyrwarl, and broader,
stepped forward and threw back his hood, revealing a
heavy face framed by thick black locks caught like Feyrwarl's in a leather thong. "What! *The* Gom Gobblechuck
who freed the cito from the solahinn pens? Master Gom,
your fame precedes you." The man stepped closer. "An
honor to meet you, sir. You must come with us, and
partake of our hospitality."

The voice, smooth with courtesy, sounded yet full of
menace. Gom took measure of the cloaks surrounding him,
of Stormfleet hovering, watchful, beyond. No gap anywhere. No chance for Stormfleet to break through either,
not without giving the game away. "I don't go with

strangers," Gom said loudly, his knuckles whitening upon the staff. "Especially those who don't give their name."

The newcomer laughed. "I am Thrulvar, leader of this company. Come with us. This wood is not safe for small wayfarers alone, however brave and fierce they purport to be."

"No, thank you," Gom said. "Now, if you'll excuse me—" There, a slight gap had opened just past Thrulvar's left shoulder. He made a dash for it, got through, only to fall headlong into a tangle of hobble bush. He had a hazy glimpse of Stormfleet rearing, preparing to rush upon them.

"No!" he shouted. "Go back! On your way!"

The cloaks closed on him, and strong hands held him fast.

"Sorry, Gom Gobblechuck." Thrulvar was laughing openly. "You're coming with us."

"Where!" Gom cried, "and why!" As if he hadn't guessed.

Thrulvar gestured to the company, who as one bowed gravely from the waist. "To the camp where our leader sits. You see, we're Yul Kinta, and our chief is Lord Urolf."

Chapter Ten

AT A WORD from Thrulvar, the party moved off into the trees. It was useless to struggle. Gom looked back, saw Stormfleet limping after them, and prayed that the cito would keep his distance, for now, anyway.

Thrulvar, catching his glance, laughed, and waved a hand at Stormfleet. "You think to fool us with that, Gom Gobblechuck?"

Gom's middle knuckled up. They'd guessed, despite the cito's sacrifice? He sucked in breath to shout warning, but Thrulvar went on.

"Use that hack to persuade us that you no longer have the cito, while all the time it lies safely out of reach? A simple trick—too simple. Lord Urolf will know its whereabouts soon, I promise you!"

Gom let his breath out slowly. Why had he panicked like that? Of course they hadn't guessed, or Stormfleet would not still be free.

The trees crowded closer; overhead was now a thick rich green, and underfoot, spires of tall fern, long since unfolded, poked up between clumps of betony and bifoil, knee deep. Gom stumped along, stabbing the ground with his staff, his lips tightly compressed. To have let himself be so taken! After Harga had warned him. And yet, instinct had told him that Feyrwarl was friend. He recalled now Feyrwarl's gasp of recognition. That one knew Harga, all right. Come to think, he had tried to warn Gom away. But moments later, he'd also declared Gom to the whole company! No, no friend, he. To think, Gom thought disgustedly, that he'd likened Feyrwarl to Carrick!

Thrulvar had spoken of a camp. Feyrwarl had said they were bound for Pen'langoth. Why? Why was Urolf going to the lakes? Not to confront Jofor, Gom prayed earnestly, not with him in the middle!

In minutes, he'd be meeting Urolf face to face. His spirits rapidly sinking, he recalled Harga's words. *They've ever been, and remain a fierce folk, quick to take offense . . .* What else? *Their powers are great . . . they see things the ordinary man cannot, their gift of prophecy is legendary, and beware of any who can look into your heart even. . . .* Anxiety sharpened into fear. Could Urolf do that? Would Gom, standing before him, betray Stormfleet's secret? Worse— the knowledge of star-gate and crystal stair? His knees began to tremble. He stumbled, almost fell.

Thrulvar laughed. "Hang on to your bravado. You're going to need it."

There came a soft call, an halloo from somewhere ahead. The company halted, exchanged greeting, in a smooth, rolling tongue. Six more cloaks stepped out to join the company, and they moved on again.

Nobody spoke, but all continued to slip with uncanny ease and silence through the trees so that Gom heard only his own boots cracking through the undergrowth. Might as well, he thought, be walking the forest with ghosts.

Fancying once or twice that he heard a soft clop some-where behind, Gom glanced back, but saw nothing be-yond the shrouded forms surrounding him.

Then, all at once, he heard talk, a snatch of song. A moment later, he passed among clustered gray tents, emerging at last into a torchlit clearing. At its center stood Urolf, amidst a company of about two score men and women.

The Yul Kinta lord wore gray-green tunic and hose that shimmered in the light, and a coronet of gold and silver leaves. He so resembled Feyrwarl that they could be brothers, but unlike Feyrwarl, Urolf looked severe and haughty—even more so as Thrulvar pushed Gom out to stand before him.

Urolf drew himself up, and folded his arms, and looked from Gom to Thrulvar in disbelief. "This stole my cito?"

"I didn't steal it!" Gom cried hotly.

"Mind your tongue," Thrulvar warned.

Urolf looked Gom up and down. "Such a brave noise it makes," he said, "for such a little thing. Just like the mother."

Gom thumped the ground angrily with his staff. "My mother is the measure of any in the world, and anyone with moth brains would know it!"

A gasp ran through the crowd, but Urolf only smiled thinly. "You claim you didn't steal my cito. How, then, did you come by it?"

"I won it, fair and square."

"*Won* it?" Urolf looked shocked. "You lie!"

"That I do not!" Gom cried. "Jofor said that if I rode the cito, it was mine. That I did, and so he had to let us go. Your quarrel, therefore, is with Jofor, for wagering with another's horse."

For a moment, Urolf looked disconcerted. Then his gray eyes narrowed. "He'd not expect the likes of you to ride it—but then he didn't know he dealt with Harga's son. You deceived him!"

Deceived him! Gom flashed into rage. "Jofor sent me to my *death!* I saved myself as best I could!"

"You'd speak thus to me, you worm, you tiny, worthless thing?" Urolf cried. "On your belly!"

Hands thrust Gom down so hard that his staff flew wide and he went sprawling. In the silence, Gom retrieved the staff, and pulled himself onto his knees, his eye on Urolf. Jofor had made Gom dance to the whip, had thrown him to the wild horses. Who knew what this fierce and furious lord might do?

"Now answer me," Urolf said quietly. "It was Harga, wasn't it? She put you up to it."

"Not true! My mother knew nothing of it!"

Another thin smile. "Oh? Then explain the skull-bird that followed Jofor's caravan over the Vargue. You think we don't know how Harga watched you do her work?"

That vile thing his mother? "That wasn't Harga! If she had wanted your cito, she'd have had it in a snap without risking her own son's life!"

"Then who, if not she?" Urolf demanded. "And"— he looked around triumphantly—"who else could pluck you from the High Vargue—from Jofor's plain sight?"

Gom fell silent. Who else indeed? Curse Jofor for his busy tongue.

"I say that even now the cito skulks in the Dunderfosse, where the Yul Kinta cannot go," Urolf said.

"Not so!" Gom cried.

"Then where is it?"

"I can't say, exactly."

"Why not?"

"Because I don't know. I—gave him leave to go his way."

Urolf looked aghast. "You gave— Oho." He looked around the company in mock appeal. "You see? Even I begin to fall for the lies and the sorcery." He jabbed a finger at Gom. "You think to hoodwink me? Then think again. We also have our ways." He raised his head. "This pipsqueak braggart shall stand before the Lady Vala, then shall we have a reckoning. Off with him."

Gom's guards dragged him to the tents, pushed him inside a small one, dropped the flap, leaving him in darkness smelling of earth and canvas. "In case you think to leave," one said, "we are four."

Gom threw his staff down, circled the tiny space, testing the rough, thick stuff of the walls, listening. A slight rustle from the other side told that his guards circled the tent also, on the outside. He subsided onto the ground, his mind whirling. Thrulvar had bragged that Urolf would have the truth from Gom. We also have our ways, Urolf had said. Who was this Lady Vala, and what was she going to do to him? Gom put his head between his hands. . . . *beware of any who can look into your heart* . . .

He looked up, picturing the high stars beyond the tent roof. *Oh, Mother. I'm scarcely out of the Dunderfosse, and in trouble already. What can I do?* Nothing, his own voice answered. He couldn't even cut his way out without the knife he'd carelessly left behind on Windy Mountain.

The canvas jiggled, and a large Yul Kinta, almost bent double, brought in a lantern, and a small tray with a bowl and a cup. His face, sour and surly, looked forbidding over the light. He was, that face said, not used to waiting on such as Gom, and not at all pleased to be demeaning himself. Without a word, he set the lantern down, shoved the tray at Gom, then ducked out again.

Gom sniffed the bowl. Grain of some sort, and leafy herb: smelled good. He sat, ate it all, took a sip from the cup. Wine, rich, red—and strong. He made a wry face, and reached in his pack for Stig's water bottle. The simple supper over, he went to the tent flap, raised it a hair.

Surly was on him in a moment. "Get back from there!" The guard pushed through, and snatched up the tray.

"Wait a minute," Gom cried, but Surly was gone.

What now? The Lady Vala? He took out the crystal, held it to the light, and turned it, looking in on his gold flake. *Mother,* he pleaded silently. *Help me.* He gazed at the rainbow shard, willing it to flash. No response. He was on his own, just as he'd been on the crystal stair. He slipped the stone back inside his shirt, folded his arms, remembering the terror of that journey: the panic, the paralysis, the sense of being unable to go forward or back. He sank down, as he'd sunk down upon that stair, and tried to think.

He was like a helpless sheep waiting to be shorn. The Yul Kinta were the many against the one. But whatever that Lady's power, he must outwit her. But how, if his mind was as a window to her, or a cupboard to be opened?

He straightened, the glimmer of an idea beginning to form. If she was going to peep into his mind, then— he'd not disappoint her. He'd fill it with safe thoughts.

Of Windy Mountain: of Stig chopping wood, of Maister Pinkle the blacksmith, of the high street and The Wild Green Man. Of Hoot Owl, and Leadbelly the tree frog, of chilly dips in the creek. Of hauling logs down the mountain, of climbing back at night with a cartload of hard-earned food. Of all that he remembered from the time before Stig's death. Anything and everything save that which must stay hidden. Could he do it? His hands tightened into fists. He must. He crossed his legs, closed his eyes, and fixed his thought on the past. . .

"Good even."

A tall, lean woman stood over him, twin black braids brushing the ground, plain robe of the shimmery gray-green tied with a thin sash. She held a copper bowl between her hands. She was alone.

Gom made to scramble up, but she waved him down again, and in one swift movement, sat and set the bowl between them. "Gom Gobblechuck, Harga's son, I am the Lady Vala."

He gazed into her eyes, and couldn't look away. She would sing fine well with that mellow, liquid voice, and she was wiser than wise. Indeed, he was sure in that instant that if he only poured his worries out before her, she would solve them for him instantly.

A voice called from outside the tent, another answered. Gom wrenched his eyes away, stared down at his boots as though he'd never seen them before. The power of this woman! No one, not Katak, not Harga, not Jastra, had affected him quite thus. . . . *their powers are great, and quite different from mine . . . beware of any who can look into your heart. . . .*

"I am here to assay you," Vala said.

"Assay?" Gom kept his eyes down.

"To test the truth of what you told my Lord Urolf this day."

The back of Gom's hands pricked. Now it would begin, now would he be put to the test. For how long? How long would he last? He steadied his thought, cast back to the old hearth of a winter night, he and Stig sitting in their chairs, toasting their hands and faces. To a small wooden rabbit, half finished, beside Stig's chair. To Stig's knife blade gleaming in the firelight, to tiny wooden shavings scattered about, smelling of pine. . .

"Gom." Vala's voice made him start. "Cup your hands together."

Stig, the hearth, the carving, everything fled at her command. Gom cupped his hands, immersed them in the bowl. He watched the water swirl over them, filling the hollow of his palms. The ripples glimmered, faded. What was he doing! He tried to snatch his hands away, but couldn't move.

She was watching him closely, he could feel her eye on him. "Don't be afraid. I'll not harm you."

Not harm him, indeed! Maybe not, but Urolf might! She must not find out about Stormfleet. *Mother, Mother, where are you! Help me now!*

Vala turned down the lantern leaving them almost in the dark. The water within Gom's hands began to glow with a golden radiance, then vanished.

Gom drew in a sharp breath. In the hollow of his palms he saw Harga quite clearly: her hair was disheveled and blowing about her face. Her lips moved, and her voice echoed through his mind. *Gom, don't give way. Hold on, remember all I told you. I trust you, I believe in you, and depend on you. Oh, my son, I feel so very far . . .* Her image wavered, steadied. She was weeping now, he could see the tears shining on her face. *Oh, if you could only see the devastation . . .*

For an instant he gazed down, linked with her in sorrow. Then his mind recoiled in horror. Not a gift, this vision of Harga, but a terrible mistake! In his fear, he'd filled his mind with her. He looked down, agonized. He wanted to go on, to see and hear more, but he must, for both their sakes, clear his mother from his mind. With all his strength he dashed the thought of Harga away, and at once the image vanished. Gom's heart filled with unbearable sadness. But—it was not all his own.

"I feel her grief," Vala said quietly. "She mourns not for herself but for whatever lies about her. And her heart breaks with longing for you." Tears spilled from Vala's eyes and ran down her cheeks.

Gom's heart twisted. Vala knew, she understood. Oh, if he could but confide in her. Tell her all. He almost spoke, almost. But something barred him. Was he not to her as Tak the raven had been to him? Someone from whom to trick the truth? Wake up, he told himself. This woman has found your weakness. Just as he had played on Tak's vanity to find the tunnel that led under Katak's island, so she was playing on his loss and loneliness in order to find out about Stormfleet. He must prevail against her. But how?

He stayed looking down at the water in the bowl, dark now, and still. Magic, Harga said, was made with knowledge and will. He had little of either. This woman had a natural gift beyond his measure, and was wielding it with consummate skill. Whatever gifts he had couldn't help him here. So what were his strengths? Well, he was stubborn. Perhaps from that plain natural gift he might just draw the power to resist.

"Don't." Vala's voice was barely a whisper. "I must know about the cito. My lord has commanded it."

Fear squeezed his chest. No, no, no! She must not! *Quickly, think, think!* She wanted Stormfleet? He'd give her Stormfleet: Stormfleet, galloping over the High Vargue. Gom on his back—*no, no!* The colt's riderless back under the stars. The horse's wild shape dwindling into the distance, blending with the other frantic, stampeding shapes. Gom began to sweat. The sweat trickled down onto his cheek, but he couldn't move his hands to brush it away. He felt his will wavering.

The water in the bowl rippled, stilled, vanished, and cupped in his hands the dark form of the cito galloped over the featureless plains. *Steady!* He felt her nudging the edge of his mind, urging him to give way. The dim and half-formed shape of Withershins gathered solidity, pressing through into his conscious thought. He pushed it away, focused on the shapes galloping in the hollow of his hands. His breath came faster, faster, until his head began to spin, as the pull of Vala's power steadily wore him down. His will was giving way . . . With one last effort, Gom pictured himself standing alone, gazing at the stampeding horses, and shouting, as he had the night he'd broken out of Jofor's stockade, "Scatter now! Go! Good speed, and good luck!"

Clinging to those images, he closed his mind to the fact that this had not been altogether so, that he'd been astride Stormfleet's back the while. No time to think, to reason, just to keep the thought steady of Stormfleet going away, vanishing across the far plain.

The light in the bowl faded, and Gom slumped, spent. He was only dimly aware that the Lady Vala lifted his numbed hands out of the bowl, dried them, and laid them in his lap. Then she took up the bowl and went out.

Gom sat, unable even to lift his head, until hands raised him, helped him out of the tent and through the camp to the clearing where Urolf waited. Gom's guides released him, left him swaying before the Yul Kinta lord. Beside Urolf stood Feyrwarl, and Thrulvar. And the Lady Vala.

"Well, cousin? What did you see?" Urolf said.

Gom snapped into life, rubbing his head clear. Vala was going to speak! Had she seen Withershins? He couldn't recall if he'd held on, or given way at last. But if he'd managed to protect Stormfleet, Vala had seen Harga, heard her speak. In a fever of anxiety, he clasped his hands behind his back and tightened them until his knuckles hurt.

"My lord, I saw the boy bidding the cito farewell, watching it gallop away over the eastern plains."

He'd held on, then? Gom trembled with relief. But he dared not rejoice. She was not yet done.

"And Harga, what of her?"

Gom ceased to breathe.

"I"—Vala glanced toward him—"did not see the cito with her."

Gom closed his eyes, he couldn't help it. She had seen his mother, had heard every word. Why did she not say? Had Vala's tears for Harga been real after all?

Urolf's brows came down. "So. Harga really doesn't

have my cito. But neither do I, thanks to her piddlesquat son." He spoke out to those around. "As Harga is a wizard, she shall make good the mischief, get me back my cito. Let four ride north and proclaim this before the Dunderfosse: two days we tarry here, two days for Harga to give my cito for her son. If by then there is no word, then he goes with us. Take him away!"

Chapter Eleven

THE NEXT MORNING, after Surly had taken Gom's empty tray, and Gom was sitting gloomily on his bedroll, Feyrwarl ducked in. "Good morning, Master Gom. I hope you slept well."

Gom jumped up. "What do you want?"

Feyrwarl smiled. "Come. Bear me no ill will. I did try to warn you."

"And then announced me to the company. Thank you very much."

"I had to, surely you could see that."

Gom surely could, and had, after long hours of sleepless night. But admit it? "Why have you come?"

Feyrwarl glanced to the tent flap, moved farther in. "To tell you how ashamed I am of my brother," he said in a low voice.

"Your brother?" As though Gom hadn't already guessed from seeing them together the night before.

"My elder by some years." Feyrwarl made a face. "I want you to know we're not all of Urolf's mind."

"Oh?" Much good that was doing him, Gom thought sourly. Still. He unbent a fraction. "I really did win the cito."

"And Urolf believes it, but he won't admit it. He's furious with Jofor for lying to him. I wouldn't be standing

in that one's boots when next they meet." He sat, waved
Gom down beside him.

"Is that why Urolf's going to Pen'langoth? To see
Jofor?"

Feyrwarl smiled. "No, Master Gom. The fact is, my
brother is in love."

Urolf in love! Gom tried to picture it.

"He courts the Lady Leana, the lake lord's sister. We
accompany him to put his suit with gifts and pledges."
Feyrwarl cleared his throat. "Urolf was supposed to have
made grand entrance on the cito."

"Oh." That, thought Gom, explained a great deal.
"What if the cito doesn't turn up?"

Feyrwarl looked surprised. "Why, won't it?"

"I don't think so."

"Well, now. That is interesting." Gom didn't offer
any more. "So I suppose you go with us." Feyrwarl rubbed
his chin. "I'll try to speak on your behalf, but don't get
up your hopes. Urolf takes little notice of me." The Yul
Kinta climbed to his feet. "Your old gray friend still
hangs about. Urolf has it driven away, but ever it comes
back. So cheer up, Harga's son. You have one good ally."
A quick smile, and Feyrwarl was gone.

Gom sat looking after him. Feyrwarl seemed to be
on his side. The Lady Vala too. And Stormfleet had
not abandoned him. Hah! That was a laugh: there sat
Urolf waiting for his cito—while sending folk to shoo
it off!

On the morning of the third day, the Yul Kinta struck
camp. Gom, his pack and staff slung behind him, rode

a pack pony in the rear of the caravan. As he rode, he looked off into the trees. Was Stormfleet keeping close? He hoped so. Never know, he thought, when the chance might come to cut and run.

For four days the company moved slowly south. A dreary time for Gom, flanked by surly guards who kept to their own tongue. Worse, he was growing stiff and sore from long unbroken hours in the saddle.

At night, he fretted, willing his stone to summon him to Harga. Fine beginning to his mission. Onder's bridge and crystal stair, indeed! The more he brooded, the more his plight weighed on him. But come dawn, his spirits rose with the sun, and anything again seemed possible. For was he not Harga's son, and his friend, the most wondrous horse in Ulm?

Urolf never came again, nor Feyrwarl either. Only Surly spoke sometimes, to give orders, or to complain. "A disgrace," he said, slopping Gom's tray down. "All this trouble for a mortal, when we have maids our lord could proudly marry."

By the fifth morning, the woodland thinned, and Gom glimpsed misty hills in the distance. Sundor's border: time to turn east, across the Wilds toward the lakes. Ten more days to Unity; Gom was keeping careful count. Ten more days to the Covenance, when the wizards would choose their new apprentices. He tried to cheer up. He still might arrive in Pen'langoth on that day. All he had to do was watch his chance and run.

At that moment, a frantic shape charged from the trees, starting the ponies, the mounted guards, scattering them. Stormfleet! Gom almost shouted his name! He leapt off his pony and ran, pack and staff bumping his back. Zigzagging like a fleeing rabbit, Gom cleared the grasping arms, and reaching Stormfleet, prepared to mount. But gray figures closed in around, seized them, and held on. To Gom's dismay, Stormfleet stood without a struggle.

"Go, Withershins!" he cried frantically. "Hup! Hup!" But Stormfleet didn't even raise his head.

Urolf rode up. "So this is why the rumpus." He eyed Stormfleet keenly.

Gom ceased to breathe. Would Urolf see? Or if not Urolf— He looked up the line to where the Lady Vala watched and waited.

Urolf turned to Surly. "Luthar, let it not be said that the Yul Kinta keep good friends apart. Since this . . . Withershins . . . is so devoted to Master Gom, then Master Gom shall ride him." Urolf wheeled and was just about to ride off when he turned back. "What is that?" He pointed to Gom's chest.

Gom looked down. In his struggles, the crystal had slipped out of Carrick's shirt. "Nothing. Nothing at all." He closed his hand about it.

"Luthar, bring it here."

"No!" Gom cried, but Luthar, forcing Gom's hand, seized it, and handed it to Urolf. "Give it back!" Gom protested. "It's mine!"

"Like my cito, I suppose." Urolf held the stone out on his palm. "You think I don't know a tool of wizardry when I see one?" He laughed shortly. "Don't scowl so. You'll have it back—when you leave. The stakes rise. My cito for Harga's son, and your stone."

When you leave!

Gom watched Urolf ride back to the front of the procession, furious. Stormfleet taken, and his crystal, all in a minute.

Luthar, grumbling, transferred saddle and bridle from the pony onto Stormfleet, the cito standing meekly all the while as though a lifetime of this very thing was what had bent his back. Gom's fury intensified. Why didn't he lash out? They'll never have me alive, Stormfleet had declared out on the plains. Let Urolf try to take me, he'd told Harga, ¬and I'll show him a clean pair of heels. Was Harga's spell still gaining power, beating the cito further down? At Luthar's command, Gom climbed heavily into the saddle, took up the reins. All his fault. All his fault that Stormfleet had drunk the potion to become what he now was. Somehow that made Gom only angrier. He wanted to seize Stormfleet's mane, to shake him to his senses. "Why?" he muttered. "What's gotten into you!" But Stormfleet might not have heard for all the response he gave.

It wasn't long before Gom got the gist of Urolf's move. Except for the recent stretches astride Stormfleet, he'd scarcely ever ridden. If he'd been getting sore on the pony, it was nothing to what he was now on this lurching, bumping bony back. For hours they ground on thus, until Gom clamped his teeth in pain. At midafternoon break he got a chance to explode. "What," he demanded, "do you think you're doing!"

Stormfleet arced his neck, gave him such a sorry look that Gom almost kicked him.

"How can we ever get away now, with the two of us here?" Stormfleet still didn't reply. Enraged, Gom hissed, "Do you know how sore I'm getting, you bumping along like that!"

"Not as sore as I am," retorted Stormfleet in a flash of

his old spirit. "Have you any idea how painful it is to walk like this for hours at a time!"

"Hey, you, up you get! We haven't all day!" Luthar was walking toward them purposefully. The company was remounting.

Gom scrambled back into the saddle, gritted his teeth, and moved on.

It was three days before Gom had another chance to speak to Stormfleet. "What were you doing, getting yourself taken?" he fumed.

Stormfleet butted his side. "Don't be so hard on an old broken—"

"Stop it, stop it!" Gom put his arms about the cito's neck and squeezed. "Sorry. I'm to blame."

"To blame?" Stormfleet brought his head around. "You know how hard it was to get captured? They kept chasing me off."

Gom looked blank.

"They keep me with the other horses. Splendid fellows. I grew up with half of them. Such a time we've had already, swapping tales about the old times."

"You let them know who you are?"

Stormfleet blew in Gom's ear. "What's the harm? Who would they tell, even if they wanted to? They're delighted at my disguise, and wish us well. Of course, they're all too far gone to want their own freedom, but they're going to help get you away. Already we know Urolf enters Pen'langoth on the very day you had in mind."

Gom looked at him in mute amazement. What wonderful news! Again, he'd underestimated Stormfleet, this time without Harga to tell him so.

The cito went on unconcerned. "He plans to have you ride in front, on my back now, I suppose, all the way into the citadel."

Of course. In lieu of ransom, Urolf would humiliate Gom, hold him up to ridicule. For Harga's benefit? But Harga wasn't here, and by keeping Gom, Urolf did more damage than he could dream. Gom frowned. Once in Scandibar, how could he break free?

"You'll escape before then, with the help of my old friends."

"You think?" Gom cheered up for the first time in days.

"Think? *I know!* Urolf rides the cream of the High Vargue, Jofor's best. How can we fail?"

The days passed. No summons from Urolf concerning the crystal. Gom had moments of anxiety. If it should flash in Urolf's hands, would it transport the Yul Kinta to the crystal stair? Or did it work only for him? He just didn't know.

As if to deepen Gom's misery, his saddle sores became raw agony. In the end, Vala came with salve and cotton bindings, to ease the hurt somewhat so that the wounds could heal.

Halfway across the barren, stony Wilds it rained, and Gom was given a Yul Kinta mantle. It was gossamer-light, and weatherproof. He threw it about himself, slung his staff and pack over it, and pulling his hood over his face, withdrew. His only comfort was Stormfleet. "Don't worry," the cito told him. "We have it pat. You and I make our break right before the citadel—"

"So late! Isn't that a risk?"

"Not according to the others. At Urolf's entry, there'll be masses of folk, so when we slip off into the crowds, we won't even be missed."

Gom looked doubtful.

"Trust me," Stormfleet said. "I trusted you."

Gom nodded. True. "All right," he said. "I will." But it was hard to go on without worrying; to sit back and let Stormfleet work on his behalf.

Four days from Unity, the rain eased and misty slopes rose on their left. The Sidliths, with their minor lakes, and steep towns cut into the foothills' granite slopes. Gom eyed the walled settlements hopefully. Inns had doors and courtyards where a body could run and hide and perhaps slip away. To his disappointment, the Yul Kinta passed the high walls by to set up camp as usual, some way off the beaten track.

Rounding the Sidliths, the procession came at last upon the Pen'langoth road, with its merchant caravans, folk on horseback, on foot; and splendid, horsedrawn carriages. Track widened into well-trodden road skirting the foothills of Lake an-Dune, and grew more crowded.

Here, standard-bearers led the cavalcade with Urolf's colors: green rowan branch against a primrose field. Folk gave way before that banner, moved aside to let the procession pass.

For three days, they progressed steadily, going with the traffic by day, camping off the road at night. Then past Hornholm, the road sloped down like an old wooden floor. The last day before Unity, by Gom's reckoning. Oh, if he could only see those three stars now! That evening the company kept going, while the traffic dwindled, and finally disappeared. The road was empty, and the sun had just set when they finally came in sight of Pen'langoth, way in the distance.

The company halted, looking down on the long lake dotted with tiny sails; Scandibar, the lake lord's island citadel hung about with many lights; rows of roofs merging into dusk. Down by the lake, past Scandibar's twin towers, above the masted wharves, stood The Jolly Fisherman where Gom's friend Carrick lived, and Essie, the landlady. Gom looked about him. Luthar one side, another just as unfriendly on the other, and more guards bringing up the rear. To be in full sight of sure haven—and hemmed in on all sides by foes. Oh, Mother, he thought. If I had just one sign, one small omen to give me hope.

Gom looked up. The first stars were out, and there, to the north, was Perelion—a hair away from Frydd and Munyr! His heart leapt. He'd asked for omen, and there it was! Tonight, up through the blind canvas of his tent, that gap would close, mystic violet light would fuse with silver, flashing into brilliance brighter than the full moon, and Covenance would begin. And tomorrow, he and Stormfleet would make their bid for freedom!

His excitement faded. His crystal—what of that?

The company made camp in the lee of a sheltered hill. Gom dismounted in a surge of frustration and waited to be led to his prison for the night. He lay on his side, thinking unhappily. When he made off tomorrow, Urolf would be so angry, he'd never give the crystal back. What to do?

There came a rustling from outside the tent. Gom sat

up in the dark, rigid, straining to hear. A waft of faint fragrance drifted in.

"Who's there?"

"Hush. Luthar's on an errand, but he won't be long. Here."

Vala. Her hand found his, and pressed something into it, something cold and hard-edged on a length of chain. "Oh, lady, thank you!" he breathed, but she had gone.

He stood, feeling the crystal warm to his hand. Vala must have taken it from Urolf at great risk. Why? Why had she helped him, a stranger, against her own cousin? Gom subsided onto his pallet. Not a stranger. Harga's son. She knew Harga, well enough to weep for her. Gom frowned in the darkness, thinking. *You'll have it back— when you leave.* Did Vala know? Had she seen what he meant to do? Whatever, she was friend, one he'd not forget.

Gom turned the stone over in his hand. He mustn't wear it. He stowed it in his pouch. Now he and Stormfleet would make their bid without a qualm.

When Gom emerged the next morning, he found the company transformed. The traveling clothes were gone, replaced by robes of silk and velvet, and jewels flashed in the growing light.

Luthar, in bright blue and purple livery, seized Gom and propelled him forth to stand before Urolf, already mounted on his bay. The Yul Kinta lord, richly dressed in white and gold with circlet of stones about his brow, bowed in mock courtesy.

"Good morrow, Harga's son. I regret your mother has

not met with my request. However, since this is for me a happy day, I give you the honor of leading our cavalcade into Pen'langoth. Luthar!"

Luthar brought Stormfleet by the halter, motioned Gom to mount.

Urolf laughed. "Hold up your walking stick, Master Gom. It shall be our standard today."

Without a word, Gom unslung his staff, raised it high, fixing the Yul Kinta with the sparrow's beady stare.

Someone laughed.

Gom eyed Urolf calmly, thinking how Jofor had also disparaged that staff before he came to grief. At Urolf's signal, Luthar mounted, and still holding Stormfleet by the rein, led him forward.

The procession had begun.

Down in the city, the sun had not as yet cleared the rooftops. Even so, the streets were already awake and stirring, folk leaving their houses to cheer the cavalcade. Twin flags waved from housetops, the lake lord's banner, silver five-pointed star on a deep blue ground: and Urolf's rowan branch. The crowd thickened, yet opened before them, leading them on. Gom, staff still high, lurched along beside Luthar, amid cheers and ribaldry.

The road ended in a square open to the water, where Scandibar reared like a stately ship, twin-masted. Two drawbridges led from square to citadel, gangplanks joining ship to shore. The farther bridge, leading to the lord's own tower, sloped steeply down from a door high in the tower wall. The nearer, public drawbridge, wide and level, led to the larger tower. It was to this draw-

bridge, manned by stiff-plumed honor guard, that Luthar
steered Gom.

Only yards to go and no sign of any disturbance. *Now.
Now.* Gom dug his knees into Stormfleet's ribs.

"Patience," the cito whickered, and kept walking.

"They're here!" a woman called from somewhere up
front.

Laughter, as Gom rode into sight. "Whoever is that!"
someone cried.

"Whatever, more like. And that awful old horse! What's
it in aid of?"

"Mayhap it's Urolf's clown mascot," a man said. "Hey!
Here comes Urolf now! Don't he look grand!"

"And rich! Look at the clothes!"

"Yul Kinta," one man spat. "Think theirselves too good
for humans. Why don't the Lady Leana wed her own?"

"Look at them horses!" another exclaimed. "Did you
ever see the like?"

" 'Specially the gray one in front, ha! ha! Hey, where's
the cito?" A man leaned out from the front line. "He's
riding his new cito today!"

"Cito?" Another man's voice. "That's no cito! That's
just a plain—"

"Shush!" another voice cut him off. "Didn't you hear
about . . ."

They were not fifty paces from the gates. "Now," Gom
urged, "now, or it will be too late!"

Even as he spoke, came a blare of trumpets.

Urolf's bay reared, twisted sideways, throwing Urolf
in his saddle. The horses on either side shied in alarm.
The crowd moved back, pressed forward again, shouting.

Panic spread, the cavalcade broke formation and all was a turmoil of neighing, bucking horses. A call from the van. Urolf was unseated! Luthar dropped Stormfleet's reins, leapt to his lord's rescue.

Stormfleet tittupped delicately sideways, was swallowed by the crowd.

Gom slid from the cito's back and led him from the square. Behind them, by the grand ceremonial state entrance to the citadel, all was total pandemonium. "Come," he said, and together he and Stormfleet wound their way through narrow twisting thoroughfares toward the fishing quarter.

The sun was up, and the air already warm when Gom finally spotted the swinging inn sign of The Jolly Fisherman. As they clattered the last stretch down the steep and narrow street to the inn, the smell of raw fish came up from the quays, and the calls of the wives cut the air:

"Salmon pink, and salmon white, salmon fat all caught last night!"

"Ee-eels, live ee-eels, long as fishing ree-eels!"

"Come buy my crayfish while you can—pick your own right from the pan!"

Coming into sight of the inn, Gom remembered the last time he'd neared it. Then, he'd jumped at every shadow, fearing it to be Zamul. They passed under the archway into the stable yard. Sunlight capped the cobbles, and the smell of hay wafted from open stalls.

The yard was empty. A quiet, safe place, haven from Yul Kinta wrath. Urolf would never find him here. Gom turned to Stormfleet. "That was well done, Stormfleet. Thank you."

"Glad to have returned the favor. Now we are even."

Gom looked around the sunny courtyard, his spirits rising. Last time, it had been full of solahinn wagons, ready to move out and back to the High Vargue. He led Stormfleet across the yard into the shade of the stable wall. Carrick would be upstairs, taking his breakfast. Who to see first? Essie, maybe, on Stormfleet's account. "Wait here. I'll be quick."

Stormfleet nodded. "Take your time," he said.

Gom peeped into the parlor where folk were already at their oatcakes and tea. No sign of Essie there. Was she in the kitchen, perhaps? He was just going to see, when a hand gripped him from behind: a large, strong hand, a hand, Gom saw to his horror as he turned his head to look, encased in wide leather gauntlet. A whip cracked and the hand whirled him about. "So. The rat comes to ground. I thought if I waited long enough I'd have you." The hand shook him savagely, rattling Gom's teeth. "Well? Have you nothing to say?"

Jofor!

Chapter Twelve

"HERE, WHAT'S THIS!" Essie stood in the kitchen doorway, in bright green satin bodice and white apron, a crock of dough in the crook of her arm, a wooden spoon sticking up out of the middle. "Put that whip down and let go that lad!"

To Gom's relief, Jofor lowered his whip and relaxed his grip, a little. "When he's told me where my property is, Miss Essie, not before."

Out came the dough spoon, and Essie brandished it over her head, advancing. "Let him go right now, or you'll not set foot in my inn again!"

Jofor, scowling, released Gom's collar. "This lad stole a most valuable horse from me, the cito that was promised to the Yul Kinta lord who even now arrives at the citadel as your Lord Leochtor's guest."

"Nay," Essie said. "You won't impress me with names. You claim this lad stole a horse, a *cito?*" She looked down at Gom fondly. "From a big man like you?" She cut back to Jofor. "If you have quarrel, go tell Leochtor. He wields the justice here, not you with that great whip!"

A muscle twitched in Jofor's cheek, but he said not a word.

"I did wonder about you turning up with your auction weeks away, and your wagons not long since refilled."Essie's spoon came up again. "Well listen here, solahinn man," she said, wagging it in Jofor's face. "Touch one hair of this boy's head and you'll not be welcome in this inn, nor nowhere else in Lakeside no more—now get you off to your plain!"

Jofor looked so angry that Gom stepped back, staff raised, his eye on the whip, but the solahinn only spun on his high heel and walked toward the yard—where, Gom thought in a panic, Stormfleet stood waiting! Would Jofor with his horse sense sniff out the truth where even Urolf had not? Gom barely checked his urge to follow.

"Huh. Good riddance!" Essie flapped her spoon after him. "Such ill-tempered men, all of them. If they weren't such good business I'd not put them up." She set down her crock and spoon and gathered Gom to her. "Where have you been, you bad boy, taking off like that? You had us worried silly, what with Jinny the chambermaid saying as how a big man in green britches was after you." She released him, stepped back, searching his face. "Who was he, and what's this about that Jofor's horse? You didn't take it, did you?"

Gom, his ear cocked for Jofor's cry of discovery from the courtyard, could scarce contain himself. "Er, only sort of," he said with an effort. "I won it on a bet." No sound. No shout, no warning whinny from the cito.

Essie's blue eyes went wide. "You did? Oh, my! Lord Urolf's cito?"

Gom nodded.

"Everybody's talking about it," Essie said excitedly. "Where did you leave it, in the yard?" She stopped in consternation. "The *yard!* And Jofor's out there! Come on!"

She took off down the hall. But Gom was out before her. "It's all right, Essie." One quick look fixed Jofor by the stable door, eyeing Stormfleet in disbelief. "I let it go!"

Jofor whirled about. "You *what?*" The solahinn advanced toward him, whip pulled back, threatening.

Gom raised his staff. "Get away!" he cried, "or you'll regret it!"

Jofor lowered his whip uncertainly, watching the staff —"little stick" as he'd called it, the night Gom had held it thus on his triumphant ride three times around the stockade. Jofor's eyes flashed angrily. "You've done the solahinn great injury. Urolf feuds with us, and through him folk shun our trading. To put things right I must have the cito again!"

"Go find it then," said Gom. Stormfleet faded into the wall.

Scowling, Jofor turned to Essie. "You're a fool, ma'am. A fool, to harbor such. He's not all he seems to be. Get rid of him, or you'll rue the day." The solahinn chief called loudly, fetched two running from the stables. A command, and they hurried past Gom and Essie indoors.

"I'll thank you to reckon my tariff," Jofor said curtly. "We leave at once." He turned on his heel and strode after his men.

Essie waited until Jofor was out of sight, then, grunting, she shooed Gom inside before her, and through the kitchen door under the eyes of startled cooks and busboys. "You stay right there," she commanded, "until we've seen yon off the premises. Corly—" she called to a small thin man in a cook's hat, stirring a cauldron over the hearth. "Gom likes oatcakes and black tea, as I recall. See that he gets plenty of both. Gom, sit!"

"But what about—" Gom called after her. Too late: she was gone. Gom sank slowly onto a stool. What about Stormfleet still standing out there, all alone? He should go back into the yard, but that might look suspicious. Best to keep clear of the cito until after the solahinn were gone—if he could only steel himself to it.

"You let the cito go and took up with *this?*" Essie tapped Stormfleet's rump in amazement. Contrite, she stroked the place she'd struck, smoothing down the rough, coarse hair. "I mean you no insult, Withershins, dear," she murmured. "But even you yourself would agree if you could but understand me that it wasn't a very smart choice." She turned away, missing the quick toss of Stormfleet's mane. "Tell me, what did the cito look like?"

Gom glanced at Stormfleet resentfully, then closed his eyes. "Glorious," he said. "Full eighteen hands high, blue-black coat, tail and mane like silk—and on his brow, the silver ringmark, sign of the cito, you know."

"Really?" Essie sounded impressed. "Tell me, what did that Jofor mean about you not being what you seemed? It gave me the shivers."

Gom opened his eyes. "Beats me up a tree," he said. And wished he could tell her at least something. That he'd been with his mother, had sat and talked and sung with her, and that she'd mended his clothes in the orchard sunshine. It bothered him, not to be open with such a good, kind friend.

Essie laughed. "You're a strange one. There's no telling the workings of your mind. But there's no bad in you, whatever that Jofor says." She nodded to the stable door. "Remember the end stall next to Finnikin's, the one Shadow sleeps in? Put Withershins there."

"Essie—" Gom hesitated. Jofor's being here changed things. Would the solahinn be angry enough to face Urolf, to offer Gom's whereabouts for peace? "Essie, Urolf brought me into Pen'langoth this morning as his captive. He paraded me in front of his procession. There was a sort of—upset and I got away. I thought to hide here without harm, but if Jofor tells Urolf he saw me, it could mean trouble." He looked down. "I ought to go."

"Go?" Essie cried. "You'll stay right here, and if that solahinn tells on you, we'll hide you fine, so where's the trouble in that?"

Gom shifted uncomfortably. That wasn't all, come to think. "Essie, half Pen'langoth saw me this morning. What if I'm recognized?"

Essie laughed. "Lad, you're in the fishing quarter. We're a close folk down here. A friend of one is friend to all. You're safe down here against Leochtor's whole army! Now get that horse settled and come on into the house. No offense, but you look sorely in need of a bath."

"Essie." Gom was overcome. Such kindness, and she scarcely knew him. "I'm really grateful. And I'll repay you in a day or two as soon as I've worked for Carrick."

"Oh, dear." Essie looked disconcerted. "I clean forgot, such a fuss as there's been. Carrick's on his summer hill round. But he's due back anytime, maybe tonight! As for you, your cot's waiting, and your clean clothes, and your pack as you left behind. Carrick said to make you easy and to look after you if you showed up—as if I wanted telling!"

"Oh." Carrick not there. Another blow. Gom jingled the tinker's money in his pocket. He couldn't stay, not without earning his keep. He pulled the coins out. "These are Carrick's. I have nothing to pay you with."

"Eh, don't you worry about that," she said.

"But I do, Essie. I do!"

At the look on Gom's face, Essie sighed. "Well . . . I suppose you could lend a hand in the kitchen. Ferd and Hathel, my two dish-hands, took off to watch that parade, and the rascals are still not back. So right now, I'm real short-handed, what with the baking, and vegetables, and delivery day, it's more than—"

"I'll start at once," Gom said. He recalled the scullery piled with dishes and pots threatening to topple.

Essie looked doubtful. "You're sure? Your bath this afternoon, then, when the rush is over?" She smiled with relief as Gom nodded, then went on more firmly, "Well, make that nag of yours easy first, then come to the kitchen soon as you like."

While Essie hurried back inside, Gom led Stormfleet down the stable to the end stall. There, he paused. The last time he'd pushed that wicket open, Zamul, in the shape of Shadow, had sprung for his throat.

Gom took a deep breath, swung open the door, and found the stall swept, and spread with fresh, dry hay. "There, it certainly looks clean and comfortable," he said, kicking through the straw.

Stormfleet stepped into that small, confined box, without a word. Gom felt quite awkward suddenly. "You'll be all right for a while?"

Stormfleet sniffed, blew out his cheeks, then put his head close to Gom's. "I could do with a rest, and I've missed Harga's grazing sorely. So go, check out your stall, and enjoy your oat pail. I'll be fine."

Gom set to work in the scullery on the piles of dirty breakfast pots and dishes. No sooner had he cleared them than it was elevenses and time to start all over, while Essie fussed, and fumed over the absent Ferd and Hathel. Even so, she tried to send Gom away, but he refused, until finally, by late afternoon, the last dish and pot were dried and put away.

Then, at last, Gom wiped his hands, took up his pack and staff from the corner where he'd set them, and climbed the attic stair. The high room was filled with sunlight, and hubbub from the busy marketplace. He crossed to the open casement and leaned out. Folk swarmed about the market, flags flapped from bright awnings, and proud sails dotted the lake. Gom breathed deep, smelling fish, hot bread, and baking potatoes. Good human smells and sights and sounds after all those days with the Yul Kinta. He couldn't imagine that snobbish folk down there! In the fall, Carrick had said, charcoal burners would toast chestnuts, and hawk bright tin pocket warmers.

Gom would miss all that. Not that he'd mind, for he'd be with Tolasin. Even now the wizard was probably coming to fetch him and then he'd be on his way at last. If not? Gom shrugged. There was Bokar Riffik. And Folgan. One way or another, he would soon be climbing up his crystal stair.

There came a tap on the door: hot water had arrived, and his bath.

After bathing, Gom went down to see Stormfleet.
"You all right?"
The cito blew through his lips. "For now." The stall was warm from the heat of his body, and smelled sweetly of horse and hay.

Gom stroked his neck. "I'd take you for a walk after dark, but I'm afraid that Jofor—"

"Don't worry. It's been a long trip. I'm glad of an early night."

Gom went back to the kitchen. Ferd, returned and looking hangdog, eyed Gom in silent awe. Essie shooed Gom away. "You've done quite enough today," she said, with a meaning glance at poor Ferd. "You rest now, and enjoy yourself, and remember that even while you're helping, Gom, dear, you're still a guest of this house."

It was too late to go see the market. Tomorrow, Gom thought, before starting work. He opted for supper in the attic, shunning the crowded parlor, even though Essie assured him that should Jofor or any Yul Kinta come seeking him, she'd know before they even turned down the hill.

While he waited for it to come, he leaned out of the casement for a view of the brilliant trio lighting up the northern sky, just the way Harga had said it would. Below, the rooftops of the marketplace were washed in pale light, mysterious radiance like a lightning flicker caught and held.

He gazed up, thinking of sky furnaces, and the Seven Realms strung like a necklace across the southern skies. If he could see them, would Harga seem nearer somehow? He took out his crystal, held it up to the dim light. When would Harga summon him? Tonight, perhaps. Tomorrow? He stared into its rainbow depths, remembering Vala's vision, the grief and horror in his mother's eyes. *If you could only see the devastation.*

Devastation.

Ruin, it meant. Destruction. And all of it caused by greed, if he'd heard Harga right. Dismas Skeller had been greedy for gold on Windy Mountain. That greed had changed him from a swindling rogue into a would-be murderer. Out of greed, the man had almost killed for it, and instead had died himself. Zamul had also been changed by that same greed from knave into cold killer. He, too, had fallen to his death. Unsavory men, both of them, but not evil, until consumed by avarice.

Gom slipped the stone about his neck and dropped it inside his shirt. Tonight, this very night, he prayed, he'd speak with Harga alamar to get and give some comfort.

A young girl brought in the tray, a girl who looked his age and height, with brown braids and soft white arms, and high, round bosom pushing out her tight black bodice. He remembered her now. She'd been in and out of the scullery all day, fetching and carrying dishes, more than the other serving maids. An odd girl, who'd blushed at his every slightest glance.

"Tell Essie thank you," he said awkwardly, aware that he didn't even know her name. "And thank you, too."

The girl, her cheeks pink, bobbed, and fled.

As he ate, he couldn't get his mind off her red cheeks, her dark eyes. He hadn't had much to do with girls. Only his own sisters, and Mudge, and Essie, and Harga, who were not girls, exactly. And none of them had ever acted in this fashion. He'd no sooner set down his knife and fork when she was back for his tray. "Missus says to tell you she's in the parlor, the fire's roaring up the chimney, and there's an empty place on her settle." The girl flushed to the roots of her hair.

"Oh." Perhaps he should go down for a while. The girl hovered in the open doorway, waiting for his answer. "What's your name?"

"Brody. Brody Leggat."

"Well, Brody," Gom said. "Please tell Essie I'll be down."

The girl fled. A moment later, Gom heard a giggle on the stair.

Essie's parlor was crowded and very noisy, and every table filled with men, big, small, lean, and large; mostly bearded and all wearing the dark blue jerseys of their brotherhood. Gom stopped for a moment in the doorway, put off by so many people. But after a passing glance and nod as Gom wove his way toward the chimney, nobody paid him further heed. Essie settled him by the chimney nook, handed him a mug of cider, then went about the room, serving ale, bandying chitchat with her customers. Gom looked around at the animated faces. Ordinary, weathered men they looked, enjoying an ordinary evening's company. But not all in that room was as it seemed. If that very moment Gom were to say Riffik's pass phrase, one of these very folk would hear it and take it to the wizard, so Harga said. He looked around again, slowly, keenly examining every face in turn. Which one? *Which one?* Agh, he could ask that question all night and not get anywhere!

He sat back, took a sip of cider, savored the prick of the bubbles as he listened to the babble in the low-beamed, alcoved room. Brody was also serving in there. As he caught sight of her, one of the men lightly pinched her cheek, smooth and soft as a ripe peach, Gom found himself thinking. She glanced up, met Gom's eye, and quickly looked away.

Essie came over, plumped herself down beside him, fanning her face. "What's this about our Brody?" She dug him slyly in the ribs. "That girl's been good for nothing since this morning!"

Gom stared at her blankly.

"Don't say you don't know." Essie laughed. "See—she's at it again!"

Sure enough, Brody was looking, but as soon as he raised his head, she turned away. He switched his attention to the flames in the hearth, feeling strange. Did Essie mean that Brody liked him? *Him?*

There came a loud snatch of song, a man jumped onto a table, banging two empty mugs together. "Let's have 'The Jolly Fisherman'!"

" 'The Jolly Fisherman'!" Voices all around took up the cry.

"Yes!" cried Essie. " 'Tis a fine rowdy shanty," she shouted in Gom's ear. "Rusef calls out the verses, and we all join in the chorus. You too!"

One man stamped his heavy boot, then another, and another, calling for the song until Rusef raised his hand for silence, and began to sing:

There was a jolly fisherman as sailed out on the
lake,
When sun did shine on water fine and gentle waves
did break.
He set out in the morning, his wooden deck upon;
He caught a hake,
And a garden rake,
And was home by half-past one.

And now the whole room joined in raucously, including Gom:

Then what did our jolly man do,
(As true as I tell this tale)?
With a jig and a grin,
He hove to by Essie's inn—
And he called for a jug of ale!

A swallow from his mug, and Rusef launched into the
second verse, after which all shouted out the chorus again.
A third verse, a fourth, Rusef sang; ten verses in all of
the rousing, rollicking shanty song with the chorus in
between.

There was a jolly fisherman as sailed across a wood,
When rain did fall in fearful squall and raise a raging
flood.
He set out in the morning, without a sign of crew;
He caught a rudd,
And a lump of mud,
And was home by half-past two.

There was a jolly fisherman as sailed a mountain pass,
When bitter breeze did quickly freeze the ground as
smooth as glass.
He set out in the morning, in boots above his knee;

He caught a bass,
And an aged ass,
And was home by half-past three.

There was a jolly fisherman as sailed along a dike,
When fog came in up to his chin—you never saw the
like!
He set out in the morning, in bonnet made of straw;
He caught a pike,
And a spotted shrike,
And was home by half-past four.

There was a jolly fisherman as sailed into the sky,
When wind did waft, an upward draft that carried him
on high.
He set out in the morning, as busy as a hive;
He caught some fry,
And a new-baked pie,
And was home by half-past five.

There was a jolly fisherman as sailed along
downstream,
When moon did glow on him below, and in the water
gleam.
He set out in the morning, as near as he could fix;
He caught a bream,
And a quinquereme,
And was home by half-past six.

There was a jolly fisherman as sailed a water wheel,
When gentle shower provided power to push him on
with zeal.
He set out in the morning, with hardtack made of
leaven;
He caught an eel,

And potato peel,
And was home by half-past seven.

There was a jolly fisherman as sailed a granite scarp,
When hail drummed past the high main mast and
scattered pellets sharp.
He set out in the morning, with empty lobster crate;
He caught a carp,
And a minstrel's harp,
And was home by half-past eight.

There was a jolly fisherman as sailed a gentle vale,
When lightning cracked and thunder racked and
stormy gusts did wail.
He set out in the morning, with miles of fishing line;
He caught a whale,
And a rusty pail,
And was home by half-past nine.

There was a jolly fisherman as sailed a waterspout,
When hurricane did lash the plain and blow the ship
about.
He sailed out in the morning, with piles of nets, and
then
He caught a trout,
And a cabbage sprout,
And was home by half-past ten.

Now everyone stood up, waved their mugs in the air,
and brought them down with a crash, for the last chorus:

Then what did our jolly man do,
(As true as I tell this tale)?
With a jig and a grin
He hove to by Essie's inn—
And he called for a jug of ale!

His face all red and shiny, Rusef jumped down, but before the room began to buzz again, another voice broke through.

"Now Dobar! Dobar hasn't sung in an age!

"Yes! Dobar, Dobar!" came a general clamor.

Essie stood up and called across the room. "Come on, Dobar. Sing us a ballad. You promised."

"Aw, Essie, that was then." Dobar didn't sound too reluctant.

"No man in Lakeside sings like you, Dobar. Come on. Give us 'Hershel and Poll.' 'Tis a treat," she explained to Gom. "Dobar warbles like a bird."

"Agh." A chair squeaked back in a smoky alcove by the far wall, and Dobar stood, broad-shouldered, barrel-chested, short neck, blue knitted boatman's cap. "I see there's no peace until I've obliged. It'll cost, though," he added, seizing his empty mug and grinning all around.

Amid good-natured shouts and assurances, Dobar took off his hat and began to sing:

They stood above the harbor looking out to sea,
out to sea, out to sea, out to sea.
Said Hershel to his Poll, "Say, when the fleet comes in,
will you then, will you then marry me?"
"Oh, yes!" sweet Poll replied,
"I'll wait upon the tide,
then I will gladly be your bride
and give my love to thee."

A deep sigh ran about the room. Gom leaned forward, intent on the burly fisherman. The melody was haunting, beautiful, sad. But it wasn't that alone that held him. Not since his father died had he heard such singing. Lighter than Stig's deep baritone, nevertheless the pure clarity of the man's voice and the depth of his feeling brought tears to Gom's eyes. Absently, he brushed them away as, in the stillness, Dobar began the second verse:

> He put to sea at sunset with the fishing fleet,
> with the fleet, with the fleet, with the fleet;
> swift gliding over waters smooth as silken sheet,
> silken sheet, silken sheet, silken sheet;
> till at the fishing ground,
> where herring shoals abound,
> young Hershel cast his nets around
> and thought of Polly sweet.

Gom, feeling eyes upon him, turned his head and met Brody's look clear across the room. As one, they both looked away.

> Come midnight, o'er the fleet crawled mist, an eerie cloud,
> eerie cloud, eerie cloud, eerie cloud;
> that wreathed about each deck and clung to every shroud,
> every shroud, every shroud, every shroud;
> and under its cold thrall
> each fisherman did fall,
> to dream of pallid maiden tall:
> gold-crowned and raven-browed.

> Now when the mist rolled on, they woke from their strange sleep,
> from their sleep, from their sleep, from their sleep;
> but of their dream enchanted did no memory keep,

did not keep, did not keep, did not keep;
save Hershel at the last,
who stayed before the mast,
still locked into the spell steadfast
upon that ocean deep.

Poll waited on the quayside, by the harbor rail,
by the rail, by the rail, by the rail;
close watching the horizon for her lover's sail,
for his sail, for his sail, for his sail;
till all at once she spied
the fleet upon the tide.
" 'Tis he! My lover's come!" she cried,
and fetched her wedding veil.

He strode up from the harbor, past his waiting bride,
past his bride, past his bride, past his bride;
to lie for nights and days up on the high hillside,
high hillside, high hillside, high hillside.
"What evil can this be,
what dread calamity
that takes my love away from me?"
wept Poll, and pining, died.

He stood above the harbor, looking o'er the main,
o'er the main, o'er the main, o'er the main;
eyes fixed upon the waters, under driving rain,
driving rain, driving rain, driving rain.
They say he leapt a-down,
and in the bay did drown,
then drifted out with seaweed crown,
and never came again.

Silence, for the longest minute.
Then someone cleared his throat, called, "A posset of
ale for the bard!"

A general murmur of assent, and the talk began again, subdued at first.

"Dear me." Essie, leaning back, dabbed her eyes. "It always makes me cry, such a sad and lovely song it is."

Gom stirred, rubbed his face, remembering evenings by the fire, songs that had brought laughter or tears. But Stig had sung of mountains, and trees, and local life. He wasn't sure he understood the meaning of this ballad. "What happened?" he asked. "Why was Hershel so changed when he came back? And why couldn't he love Poll anymore?"

"Ah," Essie said. "Ask any man here and he'll tell you something different. Some'll say as it was a mermaid as enchanted him, some that it was the sea itself. Others, that sheer wide loneliness emptied Hershel's heart of love. I myself think some sea witch cast a spell out for any as had love in his heart—and caught Hershel, with his heart full of his Poll. But that's the beauty of the song—nobody exactly knows. Only that Hershel went off into the mist and came back all changed." She shook out her handkerchief.

Gom stared into the fire, much disturbed by the song. Presently, he looked covertly across the room to where Brody leaned over a table, her back to him, setting down cider mugs. He tried to picture them sitting side by side on the settle. What would he say to her? How would she reply? And what did she expect of him? He didn't know. Down in Clack, his brothers and sisters had all made friends and in time had courted, and most had families now. But up on Windy Mountain, Gom had missed all that. Not that he'd minded, being perfectly content with his father for friend, and too young to think of girls and such. Still. Here he was, never having learned what any ordinary fellow would know, and where would he learn it now? Would he be on the outside all his life?

"Gom?" Essie was watching him. "You're much too young to look so down. Drink your cider, and I'll have you another."

As Gom obediently raised his cup, a new voice, high-pitched and rapid, piped over the general hum—a voice he'd know anywhere. Gom jumped to his feet, searching each table in turn, and there, right across the room, sat Mat, the youth from Bragget-on-the-Edge!

Chapter Thirteen

GOM CRANED HIS HEAD. Mat was sitting with a crowd of fishermen, and talking a fair lick. As Gom watched, one of the men doffed his cap, revealing a bare scalp. In response, Mat drew his fingers through his pale stringy locks, then patted his pockets. The man nodded, and held out his hand. From one of his pockets, Mat produced a blue glass bottle stoppered with a large cork. He turned the bottle around with a flourish, showing a large white written label. Mat tapped the label, then pushed the bottle at the man.

Gom's eyes widened. Mat could read and write? Well, well! Hadn't he believed in Mat all along, defended him to the folk of Bragget-on-the-Edge? He nodded to himself in satisfaction. Even though Mat had been a bit hasty, promising the villagers sure-fire remedies that went awry, he could read, and so he couldn't be bad as people reckoned him!

The man threw two silver coins down onto the table, took up the big blue bottle, slipped it out of sight. Mat produced a second bottle, slid his forefinger along the label, reading the directions slowly and clearly, then pointed at another man's throat. The second man pushed a florin under Mat's nose, slipped the bottle into his pocket, and went out.

"See someone you know, Gom?" Essie said.

Gom, nodding, pointed. "That lad over there, the tall thin one with the straight sandy hair—he's called Mat. I bumped into him up north." 'Bumped into' was putting it mildly. In his dash to flee the angry Bragget mob, Mat had knocked Gom flying, never stopping to help him up, or even apologize—but then, Gom reminded himself, there'd been no time.

"Eh, let's have him over, give him a mug of cider," Essie said. "I think we can squeeze in another skinny body." Essie sent Brody to Mat's table.

Mat was over in a flash, bowing and beaming.

"Well!" Essie eased herself up, and stood, a formidable figure, smoothing down her red evening silk hung with bugles of jet. "So you're Mat."

"Matamor Marplot is my full true name, dear lady," Mat said, then bowed again with great ceremony deeply from the waist.

"Indeed." Essie's voice lacked its usual warmth. "Well, young man, any friend of Gom's is welcome here. Sit you down and make yourself easy for a bit." She beckoned Brody over. "Cider for Gom's guest!"

Mat perched, slid back, and crossed his long thin legs. "I am indeed at your service, ma'am," he said, but Essie had gone. Not in the least put out, Mat turned to Gom, looking faintly puzzled. "You're Gom, I take it? The proprietress called us friends," he went on as Gom nodded. "While I do not deny it, indeed, I do not," Mat held out his hand to receive the cider mug, "I can't quite truthfully recall . . ."

Gom smiled. "We had a—glancing acquaintance up

north. In the village of Bragget-on-the-Edge, to be exact. When they ran you—"

"Ah, yes, my good fellow," Mat said hastily, looking around. "It comes to me now. Yes. A fortuitous encounter—and lucky too." He took a long pull of cider, set down the mug, and draped his arms along the settle back, expanding farther into Essie's empty place.

Gom watched in admiration. Mat looked so confident, so at ease, and not at all awkward and self-conscious. He slid one of his arms over the settle also, but it was a stretch, and quite uncomfortable. He quietly returned his hands to his lap.

"You with folks?" Mat asked.

Gom shook his head. "Not exactly," he said.

"Neither am I, dear fellow. You got folks? You're not from around here, I can tell by your accent. Where are you from?"

Gom thought a bit. "I'm from Windy Mountain. Son of a woodcutter," he said. "My father's dead. I'm traveling right now."

Mat laughed and clapped him on the back. "Dear fellow—my story exactly. Except," his smile gave place to a look of pain, "you can't possibly know the suffering I've endured."

"Oh?"

Mat leaned forward confidentially. "My poor mother was a herb wife. My father—" He clapped a hand to his head. "My father was a beast. Used to beat my mother, then me. See this?" He slid his sleeve up to his elbow, revealing crisscross scars. "That's nothing to the rest of me. My father was a scoundrel. He whipped me every Sunday to mark the beginning of the week. Then every Saturday to mark its end. When at last my poor, dear mother succumbed, I ran off, taking her remedies with me. I was nine at the time. I've never looked back, oh no. And now," he leaned back again, "I'm my own man. There's nothing like it, going around the countryside, doing good, dispensing healing and light for mere pennies. Being welcomed everywhere. No one breathing down your back, no more harsh words, no more whippings."

"But—" Gom recalled Mat's near flogging up in Bragget.

"Aaahh." Mat stretched his long legs out luxuriously. "For a roving body, you're doing well." He jerked his head in Essie's direction. "How did you manage it?"

Gom shrugged. "What were those blue bottles for?"

Mat looked startled. Then he smiled. "It depends."

"On what?"

"What you need them for." As if by magic, Mat produced two more blue bottles, one in either hand. "This," he said, holding up the left one, "is for the megrims. This other," he raised his right, "is for noisy chests."

Gom compared the labels closely. "What does that say?" He pointed left.

"It says, 'For the Megrims: Take One Teaspoonful at Night Before Bed.'"

"And that?" Gom touched the other label.

" 'For the Cough: Take One Level Tablespoonful under the Tongue Whenever the Chest Becomes Troublesome.' "

"But—" Gom looked from one label to the other, frowning.

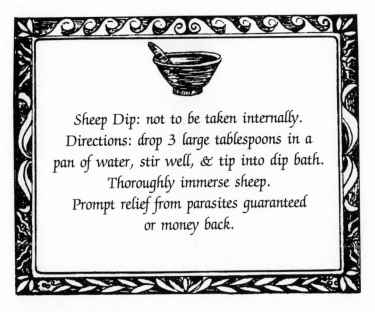

Sheep Dip: not to be taken internally.
Directions: drop 3 large tablespoons in a
pan of water, stir well, & tip into dip bath.
Thoroughly immerse sheep.
Prompt relief from parasites guaranteed
or money back.

"They look alike to me."

Mat tipped back his head and laughed. "They are, dear boy."

Gom scratched his head. "I don't see," he said. "How can the same label say two quite different things?"

"Simple," Mat said. "It says exactly what I want it to say, which is what you need to hear. Where's the problem in that?"

"But—what does it *really* say?"

"How should I know?" Mat spread his hands. "I can't read. But neither can anyone else. So when I sell cough tincture, the label's for that. When it's a cure for the megrims, it's for that. Hair restorer, for that too. And for sore throats, warts, bunions, and belly gas. Don't worry, folk remember exactly what I say, not being able to read. The thing is," Mat lowered his voice, "they're more impressed by the official apothecary labels than they would be otherwise."

Gom shook his head doubtfully. "Where did you get them?"

"I acquired a whole crate of them, bottles, labels and all, from an apothecary's back stoop. Just sitting there, they were, quite empty—obviously used, don't you know, and waiting to be thrown away. Naturally, being an obliging chap, I saved the man the trouble and expense."

"But—" Gom broke off, frowning. The labels looked quite clean and new, the corks bright and unused. Yet— why should he doubt Mat? Gom looked at his new friend uneasily. Mat could have been mistaken. . . He meant well, Gom was sure. But for all Mat's easy urbanity, Gom sensed that the youth might lack common sense and a good grounding—especially with such an unfortunate start in life. Imagine, growing up without a father like Stig to steer one in the right direction. Gom thought of all the scrapes Stig had saved him from—and all the ones that he'd gotten himself into despite that. Perhaps it was up to him to help this less fortunate soul. "Have you thought," he said, "of apprenticing yourself to an apothecary?"

The strangest expression flitted across Mat's face: secretive, and perhaps a little smug. "Oh, yes indeed," he said. "But—" He leaned forward and murmured in Gom's ear. "I have—higher ambitions." He sat back again, and went on in his normal voice. "Right now I'm looking for an assistant." He shot Gom a sidewise look. "Someone who wouldn't expect to be paid a fortune while receiving valuable free training—a lad like you, perhaps."

"Well," Gom said, flattered, yet taken aback. "I'm not sure that I—"

"Eh, then." Essie was standing over them, hands on hips, looking flushed and displeased. "What's this I hear about selling remedies in my parlor?"

The blue bottles vanished instantly. "Whoever told you that, dear lady?" Mat's face curved into a wide and ingratiating smile.

"Them two fishermen out there did," she said, jabbing a finger toward the parlor door. "There's quite an argument going on because they dropped the bottles in the hallway and they don't know whose's which! If you don't get out there now and sort it out, I'll send for Leochtor's men to do it for you!"

Mat sprang up. "I'll fix it in a blink," he said.

"You'll more than that, lad," Essie said. "Everyone knows as I don't allow selling in my house. No exceptions, no favors. I've been burned too many times. Try it again, and you'll not be welcome no more."

Mat bowed. "My apologies, ma'am. I wasn't aware of your house customs. Thank you for the cider, and good night." He looked down at Gom with a rueful smile. "It's not always easy, working for other people's welfare. But yet I go on, in my old mother's memory. My offer stands. Stall opens at nine sharp. Ma'am, Master Gom." Mat nodded to each, and bolted for the door.

Essie threw herself down beside Gom. "I hope you're not upset," she said. "But I've been hearing things about that young man that don't reflect to his credit."

"I'm not upset, exactly, Essie." Gom sighed. "But he's not as bad as folk paint him. He had an unfortunate start in life. And he's so quick, you see. That can be a drawback, for when your mind goes at such a clip, you don't always stop to think what's wise."

Essie smiled. "Love you," she said. "I know some other lad as hasn't got folks, but he doesn't go around cheating foolish people. As for the other, that young feller knows exactly what he's at, and he doesn't care about the rights and wrongs of it while there's coins falling into his pocket." She swiveled to look him anxiously in the face. "Master Gom, it's none of my affair, but I couldn't help overhear. If you're thinking to get involved with him—you'd best give it careful thought."

Yawning, Gom stood up. "Essie—thank you for the advice. I'll mind your words. And now I think I'll go to bed. What time do I start in the morning?"

"Oh, Gom, dear. You don't have to work, you know. Ferd and Hathel are back and—"

Gom's face darkened.

"Well, perhaps after elevenses, then. Give you time to go out and walk about a bit, take a turn around the marketplace." She shot him a glance. "I hope you're not thinking to take up any secondary employment!"

"No . . . o . . . o," Gom hedged. "But I promised to visit Mat's stall."

Essie sighed. "As I said, Gom dear, it's none of my business. But I'd hate to see you get yourself into trouble on that one's account. Take care."

"I will, I will," Gom reassured her, and went upstairs. Before climbing into bed, Gom craned out of the window, gazing northward. Then he looked down over the empty marketplace. Was Tolasin here? Perhaps he'd come quietly, tonight—up the back stair! He climbed into bed and lay, staring up at the silvered ceiling. Waiting was difficult, the not knowing how or where or when. For Harga. For his master to arrive. Patience, he told himself. Harga will summon you. And Tolasin will come. And if he doesn't, you know what to do.

The next morning, the cito stood in his darkened stall, chomping hay moodily. "Well?"

"My master didn't show. But neither did the Yul Kinta. You want to walk down to the market with me, stretch your legs, get some fresh air? It's not too crowded at this hour."

"I thought you'd never ask," Stormfleet stamped his foot. "Come on, get me out of here!"

Gom put the halter around the cito's neck, for appearance's sake, and led him eagerly down the hill. As he went, he couldn't help but pick up speed. He was looking forward to seeing the market again, and to inspecting Mat's stall.

Gom steered Stormfleet across the street and in and out of brightly colored tents and booths. To his delight, he came at once upon the cutler. While Stormfleet pawed the ground beside him, Gom took his time, searched the rows of gleaming blades, heavy fish knives, mostly, and found the knife he'd so admired before. He picked it up, weighed it, felt the blade edge. Small, finely balanced, light, the handle fit his palm exactly: a perfect wood knife. Gom fingered Carrick's coins in his pocket, let them be. He'd work and wait, buy it with his own efforts, perhaps even a new shirt also.

"Good knife, that. Want to bargain?" Gom looked up, found the vendor watching him. He set the knife down, shook his head regretfully, and moved on to find

Mat setting out an array of various bottles on a stall made from odd fish crates roughly nailed together, lending the display a crazy tilt. In among the green and brown and clear glass bottles shone the blue, the only ones with shiny white labels and the pestle and mortar, insignia of the Apothecaries' Guild.

"Ah! Gom! I knew you'd come. A fellow after my own heart, I told myself." Mat eyed Stormfleet in surprise. "Is that animal yours?"

"We're friends," Gom said quickly, as Stormfleet looked about to erupt.

"Interesting. Have you a cart, dear boy?"

"Oh, no," Gom said. "Nothing like that."

"Oh, well." Mat shrugged. "There's no accounting for, um." He shoved a feather duster at Gom. "Here. Start with the top row and work down. They sell much better when they shine."

"Just a minute." Gom eyed the ramshackle display. "Have you a hammer?"

Mat frowned. "A hammer? Good gracious. Somewhere. Why?"

"The first wind that blows, those bottles are going to hit the dust. I can fix the boxes, make them more secure."

"You can?" Mat eyed them doubtfully. Then he reached under a crate and brought out a rusty tack mallet and a tin of bent nails. "Here. What have I to lose?"

"Wonderful!" Stormfleet tossed and stamped his disapproval. "So much for stretching my legs!"

Mat started back. "Is it safe? Does it kick?"

"Quite safe," Gom said firmly. "Withershins," he commanded. "It's only for a little while. Mat's a friend too."

Stormfleet disdained to answer, but Gom could see he was annoyed.

Quickly, Gom removed the bottles, set them aside, and with great care, prised the boxes apart. Then, as if by magic, he reassembled them, in sturdy, level steps, and set the bottles out again.

Mat clapped his hands delightedly. "My dear chap, where did you learn to do that! How can I ever thank you? Here." He fished in his pocket, took out a small, a very small copper coin. "Buy yourself something."

Gom took it, laid it in his palm. A penny. Handsome wage for such a little favor. It would, if he recalled, buy a rather large and tasty sticky bun from a stall not far away. "Thank you, thank you very much."

"Now," Mat said, pushing the duster at Gom again. "To work. I see a customer coming already." He peered into the crowd.

"You said a walk," Stormfleet whuffled mutinously. "I'll not stand around here while you wave those chicken feathers about. I'm off."

"Wait," Gom said. "Just a while longer. I want to see how Mat does."

"Does what? Cheat honest fools out of their hard-earned money?"

A large red man in leather breeches and faded blue tunic stepped around the stall. "Are you the pothykeery?" he asked Gom.

"I'm he." Mat elbowed Gom aside. "What can I do for you?"

The man pointed down. "It's this here bunion on me foot. Can't hardly fasten me boot this morning. Got anythink for it?"

Mat wagged a finger at him. "Just the very thing, dear sir. I'll have my apprentice hand it down right away." He nudged Gom. "There it is, Master Gom. Top row, third bottle from the right. The label that says, 'Lotion for Bunions of the Foot.'"

Gom eyed the top row, thinking how Mat could reach more easily than he, counted the bottles out, and took down a blue one with a label exactly like those he'd seen the night before. He stood holding it, a doubtful eye on Mat. Bunion lotion?

"Come, my boy, we can't keep the gentleman waiting." Mat seized the bottle, ran a finger along the words under the man's nose. "It says, apply to affected area twice a day after meals. If swelling persists when contents of bottle used up, you may acquire a refill at generous discount. Thank you."

The man took the bottle, handed over a shilling, and limped off.

"Does it work?" Gom watched the man vanish into the crowd. He seemed to be in great pain.

Mat looked huffy. "I've sold forty bottles, and not one's come back. And for only a shilling each. The same would cost forty shillings apiece from an apothecary, I can tell you. Look," he said. "I still like the way you work. You're handy with tools, and you seem trustworthy enough. So I'll repeat my offer: a job as my assistant, for—"

A tall, burly man stepped up, dressed in fisherman's blue, and tapped Mat on the arm. "You sold me one of them sneezing remedies last week."

Mat leapt back. "I did? What of it?" He seemed to

have forgotten Gom. In fact, his eyes went around him, and Stormfleet, looking for gaps.

The man thrust a hand deep in his pocket. "Here." He brought out a small silver sixpence. "Cleared up completely, and never bin back!" He thrust the sixpence into Mat's lifeless hand and walked away.

"Oh, oh, my dear sir!" Mat recovered at once. "Thank you so much, only too glad to oblige!" He pocketed the silver coin, grinning. "Well, now. As I was saying, never any complaints. Where was I?"

"You were saying," Gom began, but just then, a tall, thin man with a stoop and a pale, ascetic face popped out of nowhere, produced a scroll, broke the seal, and unfurled it, eyeing Mat over its top edge. "You're Matamor Marplot, of, ah, No Fixed Abode?"

"That's my brother," Mat said quickly. "Twin. What can I do for you?"

"I think you know that," the man said. "For I seem to remember reading you this same notice on this very same spot only last year. However," he cleared his throat. "Tell your brother, your *twin* brother, that if he's not gone from these, ah, premises within twenty-four hours, the forces of law and order shall come and help him off. Got that?"

Mat looked as though the man had shoved a bad fish under his nose. "My dear sir—"

"Hey," Gom said. "Who are you, and what right have you to tell my friend what and what not to do? He's not hurting you, and he's nothing to do with you." Mat tugged at his sleeve.

The man looked down his long thin nose. "This, ah,

gentleman's brother is a vendor of, ah, quacks and nostrums. I have here a list of complaints that have been put before the Guild of Apothecaries. Besides which, don't you know, it is against the law to dispense remedies and emollients in Pen'langoth for profit without certification? Last year, I had four of these scrolls, full of complaints against him. 'Tis a wonder he wasn't strung up from the highest mast in the harbor."

"Oh, really," Gom said, folding his arms. "Well let me tell you that he's sold forty bottles of bunion remedy alone, and not one's come back. Furthermore," Gom warmed to Mat's defense despite frenzied tugging on his sleeve. "A man just came and gave, yes, *gave* my friend— my friend's brother—twin brother—a sixpence, a whole *six*pence extra for curing his sneezes! So you just mind what you say about quacks and such!"

The man stared, speechless for a moment. Then he rolled up the scroll, and leaning down, put his face close to Gom's. "You're new around here, yes? Well," he went on, as Gom only continued to glare, "I daresay you've never heard of honey-thumbs, have you?"

"Honey-thumbs?"

"Pacifiers, young fellow. As with the honey a mother sticks on her baby's thumb to stop its squalling." He shot Mat a contemptuous glance. "The poor fool who just now parted with sixpence more than he should have—he cured himself." The man tapped the side of his head. "A glass of lake water would have done just as well—which is probably what he bought." He turned to Mat. "Twenty-four hours, tell your brother. After that, the law will be around to help him off." The man rolled up the scroll and walked away.

"Well!" Gom exploded. "Of all the rudeness. Why didn't you—"

Mat cut in. "That's all right, dear chap. All I do is pick up my display and move to the other end of the market—for as long as I'm here. I'll pay you a shilling a week—a fair sum, as you'll find out if you ask around. The only thing is, you might turn up one morning and find me gone."

"Gone as in Bragget?" Gom looked to where the tall thin man had disappeared.

"Good gracious, no." Mat flapped a disparaging hand in that direction. "Don't pay him any mind. The fact is, I have higher aspirations."

"Oh?" Now Gom recalled hearing Mat say the same thing last night. "Like what?"

Mat looked around at the folk drifting into the market-place, and lowered his voice. "Right now, at this very minute, is a time certain folk call Covenance. You wouldn't guess it, but not far from here, in a very secret place, certain people are gathered to make great decisions, and to take smart and able young bodies in order to teach them—oh, all kinds of secret things." His voice became earnest, almost intense. "I daresay this doesn't make much sense to you, but believe me when I say that very soon I shall be embarking on a mission such as would set the good folk in this marketplace on their ears!" He looked around again, then went on. "As you've been a friend, a good and loyal friend, why, if I'm lucky, as I'm sure I shall be, then perhaps I shall be able to do you a favor, a bigger one than you could ever dream."

Covenance! Did Mat mean to become a wizard too? Yes, and to help him also, if possible. Now there was a friend for you! "Why," he cried, "are you going to be a—"

Stormfleet, who'd stood listening all this while, reared up now, neighing loudly. "Are you mad? Hold your tongue!"

Mat backed into his display, rattling his bottles. "That beast—dear boy, he's quite wild. I must insist—"

Gom didn't hear the rest, for at that minute, Essie burst through the crowd, her chest heaving as she strove for breath. Gom looked at her in surprise. Her ample presence seemed shrunken out in the open market, and not nearly so overwhelming as in her own domain.

Mat's jaw dropped in consternation, but she gave him not so much as a glance. "Master Gom!" She took Gom's arm and pulled him away, in the opposite direction from the inn, some distance from Mat's stand. Gom let himself be drawn, Stormfleet clopping behind, until she stopped, and spread her hand on her heaving chest. "I ran the moment I saw them!" She glanced back through the crowds toward the inn street.

"Yul Kinta?" Gom's flesh pricked.

Essie nodded vigorously. "Four, and Leochtor's soldiers with them. We've got to get you away—and quick!"

Chapter Fourteen

GOM GRABBED Stormfleet's bridle. "Get us
where?" he said.

Essie glanced back the way she'd come. "To
Cousin Hannan on the dock, come on."

Cousin Hannan? Gom eyed her doubtfully. On the
dock?

"He's a boatman," Essie said. "Good, and solid, like
Carrick."

Gom hung back. "What about Withershins? Can he
get down there too?"

"I'm sure, if he treads careful. Now come on, Gom
dear, before they're here looking for you."

"Go," Stormfleet whickered quietly. "I'm with you."

Gom stood on tiptoe for a last glimpse at Mat, but
friend and stall were both gone behind the crowds. So
he turned and led Stormfleet after Essie down toward the
dockside, coming at last to the open fish mart, rows of
low stone slabs piled with slippery wet fish: trout, salmon,
carp, and bass. The smell was overpowering, and the
noise. Buyers milled about with baskets, leaning across
the stalls, poking, inspecting the catch. As they went,
greetings came on every hand, and curious glances at the
horse. Essie answered all with a finger on her lips. A
quick nod and a wink, and the greetings, the glances
stopped. "Let that Urolf search the market all he likes,"

Essie reassured Gom. "He'll learn nothing now that he shouldn't."

They reached the lake front, an ancient boardwalk connecting docks of all odd lengths and heights that poked out into the lake like teeth on a broken comb. At the head of each dock swung a sign: a leaping trout, a crayfish, a net, a rod and reel. Essie led Gom past the docks, and the tethered fishing boats bobbing in the waves, right down to the end of the boardwalk, fetching up at last before the sign of a barbed hook.

"Here we are." Essie took Gom's arm. "Watch your step. And mind Withershins: the boards are bad."

Gom led Stormfleet carefully over loose, weathered planks between which he could see sunlit pebbles on the lake bottom, sloping down into the depths. Shoals of tiny needlefish started under their moving shadows, shot out into the tide. Wind lifted Essie's skirts, tugged playfully at Gom's hair, but Gom, unamused, only clutched his shirt front, shivering in the sudden chill.

A large, graceful sailboat gently bumped the end pilings. From the prow rose a carving, a barbed hook big as Gom, painted blue. On the end of the dock stood a shed, against which were stacked empty baskets and crates, and nets spread to dry in the sun. Essie went to the shed door, rapped three times. "Hannan? It's Essie. Open up, quick."

A click of heavy latch, and the door swung inward, revealing a tanned and grizzled head, and inquiring eyes, blue as Essie's.

"Gom, dear, this is Cousin Hannan Whitlock." Essie turned to Hannan. "Cousin, Gom's in a parcel of trouble.

Leochtor's men seek him, through no fault of his own. Will you hide him here?"

"Leochtor's men?" Hannan looked thoughtfully from Gom to Stormfleet, and back to Essie again. "I expect so," he said slowly at last.

Essie threw her arms about him. "Oh, Hannan, thank you. I knew I could count on you. Where can we put Withershins?"

"Well, not in here," he said. "There's barely enough room for me. How about tying him up under the winder, on the lakeward side."

"Sounds fine," Gom chipped in quickly, heading off any possible affront. To his relief, Stormfleet suffered himself to be led around to the back of the hut and tethered to a hook under the window, while Hannan filled a water pail and set it down. "There." Gom patted the cito's back. "The air's a bit fresh, but at least you can't be seen from the shore."

Stormfleet snorted. "This is nothing to the winds over the Vargue. Go about your business—and don't let that female forget my creature comforts!"

Wind snatched Essie's hair, blew it in her face. "Eh, look at this!" she cried. "Let's get inside!"

The three of them crammed into the hut, Essie, Hannan, and Gom, and shut the door behind them. The inside was dimly lit by the one small smoky window overlooking the lake, which now framed Stormfleet's head. The walls were hung with nets and glass floats and coils of rope, and the smell of fish was thick.

"It's so good of you, cousin, dear. I'd stay if I could, but I'd better go afore I'm missed." Essie turned to Gom.

"I'll send along some bits and pieces as soon as it's dark—not forgetting oats for Withershins. I wish I could bring them myself, but it might not be wise." She paused in the doorway. "Whatever shall I tell Carrick if he comes?"

"Everything," Gom said. "He'll understand."

"I know. I only wish he was here right now. Got to go. Take care, you hear?" She fled out the door. Gom listened to her footsteps clattering off along the dock.

Hannan ducked his head at the window. "That horse of yours going to be all right?"

"I think so," Gom said. "He'll just have to be, for now, won't he?"

"Hummm," the fisherman said after a minute. "How about you?"

Gom looked down at piles of net at their feet. "What were you doing when we came?"

"Mending these, lad, and setting them out in the sun to dry."

"Then show me how," Gom said. "For I can't sit counting thumbs all day."

Gom stood by Stormfleet in thick, dark, mist, ears straining. It was almost an hour since Hannan had gone to look for Essie's errand boy. They were to stay by the hut, Hannan said. And at any hint of trouble, Gom was to get Stormfleet up the gangplank and onto the boat. Gom looked across the dock to where the craft rose and fell with the gentle movement of the night water.

"Hide on a dock, hide in a boat—when we should be in plain sight at The Jolly Fisherman. How will Tolasin find me, Stormfleet?"

Stormfleet rubbed his head against Gom's shoulder. "Any self-respecting wizard will have the means." He pricked his ears. "Your fisherman's back. And not before time. My barrel's hollow."

Sure enough, boots came crunching over the uncertain planking, and a moment later, Hannan loomed out of the dark, laden with bags and bedding. Gom took some from him, and followed him into the shed.

Hannan dropped his load heavily to the floor. "That Essie—she's sent enough vittles to feed an army—a mounted army—for a month!"

"Did she say anything about Yul Kinta?" Gom retrieved a large bag of oats for Stormfleet.

Hannan grunted. "They've gone, but Leochtor's men are still about." He took down his boatman's cap from the door. "I have to go," he said. "I'm behind the fleet as it is. Feed your horse, and yourself. And keep close. You'll be all right until morning? My offer to take you out still stands."

"Thank you, but Withershins doesn't take kindly to being on the water. If any come looking, we'll just leap off the dock and swim for it!"

Gom watched Hannan climb aboard the boat, pull in the gangplank after him, hoist the sail, and slide like a ghost vessel into the fog.

Stormfleet stood contentedly, his head down into his oats. He popped up long enough to send Gom indoors. "Look to your own nose bag. You must be as hungry as I am."

Gom went in and inspected Essie's packages. She'd

surely done him proud: potato pie, brown beans, baked barley, with crusty bread and hard salt cheese. Apples, cherries, and plums fit to burst in the mouth!

Gom ate a bit of everything, then lay back, hands clasped over his middle, listening to the comfortable sounds of Stormfleet drinking from his pail. He turned his head, stared up through the tiny smoky window.

So many worlds within worlds, even on Ulm itself. Somewhere in the deep and mystical Dunderfosse was Harga's close and secret world, vacant now, save for Jilly the goat. Out there, beyond the hut, past the fish slabs and above the market square, Essie and Brody were minding their bright and homely world. Yet not too far away lay another, secret world of the Covenance.

And none of these worlds had any idea of the distant Seven Realms, of the Tamarith-awr-Bayon, and the deadly force that lay locked in yet another secret world, the deep cave under Great Krugk.

Lying in that shed, out on the water, Gom felt strangely remote from them all. Cut off. Yet not afraid as on the crystal stair, because he lay among simple earthy things with simple earthy smells of hemp and wood and lake fish, and Essie's new-baked bread.

He took out his stone, held it in his hand. If only, he thought, if only he could speak to Harga now. He sighed, and rubbed his face. He shouldn't give way, he knew. His mother must have it worse than he. But it would be much easier to carry on if he could see her, even for the briefest while.

He stared into space, and presently began to hum softly, then to sing.

If I could but know where Harga has gone,
and the day of her returning;
If I could but learn she misses her son,
and her heart is touched with yearning:
But I only know for now I must go on,
Up the dark, uncertain steps blindly;
Walk the high and narrow stair, till I have done,
Leave my world familiar behind me.

He tried to picture the crystal flashing, his going to the sky hall, finding Harga there, waiting. *Oh, Mother.* Twenty-seven days since their parting—for him. Time was so different up there, she'd said. It could be only a day for her, or even hours . . .

His eyes began to close. Such a long day, it had been, as days are when one is watching and waiting and cooped up in the one small space. His hand uncurled, releasing the stone to lie against his shirt. He was just slipping into sleep when a lightning flash brought him upright. Lightning? On this misty night? Half-filled with sleep, he looked around. The flash came again.

The crystal! Gom blinked against the dazzle. Another flash, and another. Keep calm, he told himself, and just do as Harga said. Gom put the stone between his palms and pressed them together, and all in a minute he was engulfed in a shower of golden sparks.

Gom came to standing, bent over, the crystal still clutched in his hands. He straightened slowly, waited for the dizziness to pass. Here was the mist, as before: light, and clinging, beading his skin, his hair.

Mist, and silence.

He hung the stone about his neck, slipped it inside his shirt. What now?

"Gom?" Harga's voice came clearly in his ear, just as Jastra's had.

"Mother!"

"Come forward, Gom."

Gom obeyed cautiously. Even so, he almost tripped against the stair. He started up, thinking of Harga waiting at the top. A dozen steps, and the fear was back. You're not really here, he insisted. Only alamar. You're still lying back in Hannan's shed. He went on up, and up. His blood started pounding, his breath came fast. He faltered. He wasn't going to make it.

"Gom, keep going. We haven't long."

I can't, he thought. *It's just like before.* But it wasn't. Harga was up there, and time was of the essence. He climbed on, his mind fixed on Harga, and somehow the fear, the dizziness passed. Almost before Gom knew it, he reached the sky hall. He ran along the passage, and out into the wide space where this time not a tree, but the true Tamarith soared in all its crystal glory, surrounded by its twelve pools of wild blue fire.

"Mother!" She was waiting in the light beam. *Alamar.*

They faced each other through the strange invisible barrier that surrounded the Tamarith; two insubstantial phantoms, however real they seemed. She looked chalk white in the brilliance; drawn, and distant, as she'd done in his vision, and her eyes still held whatever horrors she had seen. Gom ached to touch her, to banish her strangeness, to bring her back to himself within the comfort of her dry embrace. As though she'd heard, she reached for him.

"Gom, my dear." It was no good, her eyes said. How could they touch, when they were not really there? She let her arms fall.

"I—I saw you."

"I know. I saw you too." How? her look said.

"The Lady Vala."

"Vala!" Her eyes widened. Then her mouth twitched. "So Urolf found you after all. How come?"

He told of his meeting with Feyrwarl, how the others had captured him.

"Pity. If Feyrwarl alone had found you, you'd have gone without harm. He's a friend, remember that, Gom. Vala, too. We three have traveled miles together. What happened then?"

Gom told of his audience with Urolf, and how Vala had read his thought. Harga shook her head solemnly. "Lucky that she was by. Others would not have been so kind. You're not still in Urolf's hands?"

"No." He told how Stormfleet had gotten himself captured, and planned their escape with the help of the other horses. When he described the fiasco in front of the citadel, Harga burst out laughing.

"Oh, dear, Gom. That I would like to have seen." She wiped her eyes. "Hold on to Stormfleet. He's one treasure. I don't have to warn you to beware of Urolf. He'll be sore as a hornet. Now tell me, where are you now?"

Gom told of Jofor, how Yul Kinta had come for him that morning. How Essie had helped him hide. "So there I lie on Hannan Whitlock's dock, goodness knows for how long. What to do about Tolasin?"

"He'll find you, don't doubt it—if he seeks you." She fixed her eye on him earnestly. "Keep careful count of the days. If he doesn't show, move fast with your first pass phrase as soon as the way is clear."

"What about you, Mother? How is it?" Bad, he could see from the change in her face.

"I'm on the Third Realm. They're holding the line before the Fourth Realm star-gate, but it's slipping. I've been over there, and, oh, Gom—"

"Devastation, you said."

"The Fourth Realm boils with hate and blood feud among the ruling houses. If we can't stop them, then Karlvod will have the gate, and move one Realm closer to Bayon."

"And Ulm."

"Yes."

Gom thought of that same devastation on Ulm, Katak or his brethren loose among the people. It would be easy enough. A lost cito had caused bad blood between Urolf and Harga, even now, without any help from outside. He couldn't imagine what all the different folk might do if set against one another by a Spohr. There'd be no shortage of Zamuls, foolish folk eager for quick profit, open to promises of power unearned. He frowned. Those starfolk must not bring their quarrel here. "Can't the Spinrathe on the Fourth Realm see what's happening? Can't they stop all the fighting, and pull together against the common enemy?"

"They can't see one. The Spohr are very subtle. I've seen the results of their work. That Realm is in a turmoil of fear, and greed, and suspicion, according to Karlvod's plan. I've seen him, Gom," she said quickly. "Only a glimpse, alamar."

"What's he like?"

She shrugged. "Like a Spinrathe, Gom. Like Jastra, maybe a bit shorter. Do you know, they were best friends as boys. They shared the same lessons, and pastimes. They lived as brothers. Even after Jastra became overlord, Karlvod was his closest ally, and second only to him in the commonwealth."

"What happened?"

"I'm afraid he got the very disease he now spreads across the Realms: greed, the lust for power. I thought, even when I saw him, that I might—" She looked down. "I don't think there's anything I can do."

"Then how to stop him, Mother? You'll fight the Spohr?" Even as he said it, he didn't like the sound of it at all. Hadn't Jastra said that only if he and Harga combined against Katak alone they might, only might, prevail. There were two of the creatures up there!

"I cannot go against the Spohr right now, my dear. Not directly. Not until I know more about them. But with my magic I'll begin to make a small stand against the madness that prevails in Spinrathen minds. That at least I can do, and must."

"Yes." As he must do his part down on Ulm. "Mother, we'll talk again?"

"Oh my dear, I hope so. For I need to see your face as much as I hope you need to see mine." She looked away suddenly, then back. "I must go. Listen—"

"Wait!" Gom said loudly. "When I am a wizard, what then? Do I come to you there?" He wanted to go right that moment, to be with her, at her side.

Harga's shape wavered, steadied again. ". . . can but do . . . one thing at a time. When you hold the Covenance's scroll of necromancy, then you'll climb this stair, not alamar, but for real. Then you'll learn at last the trust that Jastra would vest in you. Until then, be patient. It is mainly hard for us all . . ." Her mouth continued to move, but no sound came.

"Mother, not yet! Don't go yet!" Gom cried.

Harga disappeared.

Chapter Fifteen

FOR SIX DAYS MORE Gom hid in the little hut; a tight, trying time of waiting. While Hannan slept, as he did in the afternoon, Gom sat on the edge of the dock beside Stormfleet, dangling his legs over the water.

"Cheer up, Master Gom," Stormfleet said on that sixth day. "He'll come tonight, I feel it in my bones."

"Umphmn," said Gom, staring down at the bright stars dancing on the lake's surface. He'd said nothing about his visit alamar with Harga, for he couldn't yet bring himself to speak of it aloud. But he stared into the crystal many times, Harga's words ringing around and around in his head. . . *When you hold the Covenance's scroll of necromancy, then you'll climb this stair, not alamar, but for real. Then you'll learn at last the trust that Jastra would vest in you . . .*

He jumped up, and paced back and forth the length of the shed. Patience, she'd also said, but it was hard. Only seven more days to the end of Unity—and of the Covenance. What was he to do?

"Calm yourself," Stormfleet said. "You can't do a thing but wait. Even if this master doesn't come, you can hardly go back to The Jolly Fisherman with Leochtor's soldiers marking every corner."

"You can talk!" Gom snapped. Stormfleet was in one of his rare good moods just then, being full of oats and sunshine. But a few times, the cito had gotten so restive that Gom had feared he'd just go off and leave him.

That night it rained, a gentle drizzle from a windless sky.

Gom sat glumly in the shed, leaving Stormfleet to doze.

The rain changed to fog, smothering the air. Gom was just thinking of taking a walk up the dock when a faint noise outside brought him to his feet. He went to the door, opened it a slit, and peeped out. "Stormfleet?" The cito was deep in sleep already.

A misty lantern hung on a pole, casting a little pool of light on the dock. He had heard a noise, he was sure. Gom looked across to the empty mooring. Not the creak of boat's timber. What then? A moment later, with a clatter, a lump of gray fur leapt from a pile of broken baskets right by Gom's foot and streaked away along the dock.

Gom cried out, then began to laugh. A dark gray cat, dockside scavenger, seeking its supper! Sheepishly, he went back inside and shut the fog out. A cat! He peered through the hut window at the sleep-bound cito, then remembered his walk. Agh, he didn't feel like it now. He was turning from the window, when the noise came again. The cat was back, no doubt, the hungry thing. It had looked rather bony, come to think. "Hold on," he called. "I'll scrounge you something." He foraged about, broke a piece of Essie's stiff salt cheese, then threw open the door to toss the tidbit out—and found himself face to face with a man.

He wore a long, dark mantle with hood thrown back. His wispy hair, haloed silver against the dock light, fell to his shoulders. In his hand was a tall staff, taller than Gom, and its tip gleamed gold.

"Well? Are you going to keep me standing on this doorstep forever?" The voice was *old,* wavery, yet with an edge that brooked no argument.

Tolasin!

Gom opened the door wider and stepped aside. Only when the old man had crossed the threshold did Gom collect his wits. He hurriedly closed the door and pulled out Hannan's stool. "Welcome, sir," he said. "If you would care to sit . . ." He gestured with a half-bow, not quite sure what was expected of him.

The wizard sat in one smooth movement, laid his staff down beside him, and clasped his long thin hands on his lap, and as he did so, the folds of his mantle fell apart, revealing a robe of gray stuff underneath.

Tolasin turned his face toward Gom, a face all highs and hollows: deep-set eyes, sharp bones, sunken cheeks; thin nose, keen as a blade. The mouth and chin, Gom saw, were covered in wispy, silver beard. "So. You're Harga's son." Tolasin pointed to a nearby pile of sacks. "Sit, *sit!*" he commanded. "You make me feel quite restless, standing there, dithering. That's better." His voice softened as Gom sat with a bump. "So. You want to become a wizard."

"Yes, sir." Tolasin certainly got to the point.

"Ummm. The thought is tempting, considering your credentials. And yet I wonder . . ." The wizard paused. ". . . why your mother isn't teaching you herself . . ." Another pause, that lengthened painfully. "She seemed strained," Tolasin went on. "She's all right, I hope?"

"Oh, yes," Gom said quickly. *At least I hope so,* he thought.

"Your mother told you how long it takes to make a wizard?"

Gom looked up again. "Seven years, she said."

"Precisely." Tolasin's silver head bobbed up and down. "Until Perelion comes again. Of course, she'd want you to come to me. She was my apprentice, you know."

"Yes, sir." Gom could see now the gleam in Tolasin's eye. He got a sudden feeling that the wizard had decided to like him. His spirits rose. Would they leave now?

"Willful," Tolasin was saying. "She was always so willful and inclined to pranks. But quick—a joy to teach! One forgave her much. Other apprentices? Scratch them, and what do you find? Ambition, lust for power: the desire to devour their masters whole. But not Harga. With her, magic was the thing. She wanted to *know.* Anything. Everything. This whole world delighted her, and all its secrets. No time for politicking, fixing who got this rank and who got that in the Hierarchy."

"She said she was a maverick, sir."

"Umph. The Elders didn't take to her. She wouldn't play their games, you see. Worse, she could dance rings around every last one of us in the end—and they knew it! Of course, she passed her finals with flying colors— top scholar of her year. So she got her scroll—but not a place in the Hierarchy! They dodged that one most ingeniously: created a separate Order for her. The Brown Order, I expect you know. She's still the only one in it, as I'm aware." He laughed shortly. "Rotten trick, sending her out without even a starter's staff. Nothing but her final certificate. Sort of, we can't bar you, but we won't boost you, either. Banned her from dealings with the rest of us. I was so disgusted I've scarcely sat at a Covenance since." He leaned forward, tapped Gom's knee. "Not that that stopped my respected colleagues from calling on her help now and then. I'd like to know who hasn't consulted her on the quiet over the years." The old man fell silent, for so long that Gom began to wonder if he'd not been forgotten. But suddenly, Tolasin spoke again. "You look just like her."

Gom nodded, not sure what to say.

"I'm sure we'd get on fine."

"Oh, sir! So am I!" Gom set his feet to stand up.

"So it's a pity I can't take you."

"Can't—"

Tolasin's beard flew from side to side. "If only I could have spoken with Harga directly, I could have told her, saved her—and you—all this trouble—and me an arduous and hasty journey I had not planned to make," he added severely.

Gom sat numb.

"The place where I live these days is not right for growing bones. And if your mother knew of it she'd be the first to agree. Besides which, I can't do right by you at all. You see, as well as magic, a master must teach the ways of folk, what makes them what they are, how best to serve them, or have them serve you. I can't provide that learning now. I've given up my practice; I don't do public fieldwork anymore."

"But, sir," Gom began. Surely there was some way.

Tolasin shook his locks vigorously. "No, young man. You must set your sights elsewhere. Now if I know Harga, she's given you other names to try."

Gom pulled himself together. "Yes, sir."

"Well, who? *Who?*" Tolasin's voice was going sharp again.

"Bokar Riffik, and Folgan."

"Hmmm." Tolasin pulled on his beard. "You'll apply to Folgan first, of course. I'm sure she told you that. Though I doubt he'll have you. Folgan has no love for Harga. She told you that, also, no doubt?"

"She did say they were not on good terms." Gom's chin went up. "But she also said that Folgan was just, and that he'd likely take me on my merit."

Tolasin's brows lifted. "She said that? It's more than he deserves! Well, she may be right, though I doubt it. Now, as to that other name. Umm. Not one I'd have chosen, but I daresay Harga has her reasons. Well, my boy: you have two choices to fall back on. Now let me see. . . The Covenance is half over."

Gom saved his breath. If Tolasin had found this hiding place, he would also know its reason.

The old man stood, leaning on his staff. "I think you are too anxious, my boy—a somewhat painful fault, and an unnecessary one, for you also have a knack of bending things your way, in the end. Be easy. You still have six nights left in which to act. Tomorrow, Urolf returns home, and Leochtor will drop the search. After all, the quarrel is not his." He made for the door, then turned back again. "You'll see Harga soon?"

Gom hesitated under the old man's keen gaze. "Perhaps. I hope."

"Very well, then." Tolasin fished in a deep pocket somewhere in the back of his robe. "Tell her that I found this a month ago." He opened his hand. In his palm lay a tiny silver snuffbox, exquisitely made, with miniature hinges and padlock and all. And on the lid was embossed a skull. "Mean anything to you?"

Gom couldn't take his eyes off it. There was no mistake. The same design had been on Zamul's bracelet: a replica of the death's-head.

Katak's sign.

He forced himself to look up. The old man's eyes were lost in shadow.

"Where did you find it, sir?"

"Aha! So you recognize it." He cocked his head to one side. "I thought you would. In fact, I wouldn't be at all surprised if that's not what Harga's at right now. Don't look so alarmed, my boy," he went on, "I can keep a still tongue—where do you think Harga learned that, eh? Neither will I ask any questions. On the contrary, I'll tell you this: I got this box off a man who tried to waylay me in the Wilds. Me! I took him for a vagabond, thinking to rob a harmless old man, you know? But I've had second thoughts since. You see, I had money on me. And I—produced—other baubles to distract him. But he wanted only my ring." The old man stuck out his right hand. On the fourth finger was a dull brown cabochon, carved with many signs. "My runestone, boy. The repository of much of my life's work. He demanded it by name—before he died." Tolasin stowed the snuffbox away. "I'm sure it means something. I don't know what, yet. But I had a feeling your mother could tell me." He went to the door. "Give her my regards, and tell her I said take care."

He was through the door in a flash, and, before Gom could stir, had closed it behind him.

Gom ran to the door, wrenched it open and looked out. The old man had vanished into the fog. He ran around the back of the hut, found Stormfleet still deeply asleep. The old man's work? Gom wouldn't be surprised, for the cito didn't stir even when Gom patted his side. He went back in, and sat down on Hannan's stool, chin on hands, too stunned by the sight of the snuffbox even to think of his own predicament just then.

It had all happened so quickly. There he'd been, falling over himself not to say anything, and then there was the little thing in the wizard's hands. Oh, if only Harga had been here! He didn't know Tolasin enough to guess what the wizard thought. He didn't know enough about anything.

Before Gom had trapped Katak under the Krugk, the Spohr had recruited Zamul to help him find precious stones. With those stones, Katak was to make magic powerful enough to find the crystal stair and breach it. He'd taken Ganash's careful hoard, then, sniffing out Harga's rune, had set his sights on that. And what a find that would have been over raw and uninvested stones, for Harga's rune had in it more power than any other on Ulm, even Tolasin's ring. But now— Gom folded his arms about himself. It seemed that Zamul had not been the only one Katak had touched. Another had tried for Tolasin's ring—and perished in the attempt.

How many more might there be out there, still doing Katak's bidding, even with Katak locked away? He took off his crystal, put it back in his pouch. How many might be here, in Pen'langoth, drawn by the Covenance as flies by honey? Maybe he'd speak with Harga again soon, tell her of this thing. Knowing of it, she might come home . . .

Only now did Gom think of his own situation.

So Tolasin wouldn't take him.

Tolasin also had said he was too prone to be anxious. Well, Gom thought, sitting up straight. They'd see about that. Six days, and Tolasin said Urolf would leave on the morrow. In only a day or two, then, Gom would be back in The Jolly Fisherman. Plenty of time to send word out for Bokar Riffik.

Yes, he nodded in the dimness, and then he'd have his wizard at last.

Chapter Sixteen

A T DAWN two days later, Essie sent word. Urolf
had gone, and Leochtor's lookouts: it was safe to
return.

"Skies be praised," Stormfleet snorted, tossing his head
and stamping his foot. "You were becoming impossible
to live with!"

"Speak for yourself," Gom said, yet smiling all the
same. They were on the move again, and he'd hardly
given way to his anxiety at all. Hardly.

Hannan walked them to the end of the dock. "Pity
you never tried out your sea legs," the fisherman told
him. "I've grown used to you. Give Essie my love, and
tell her I'll be coming in for supper any day." Hannan
patted Stormfleet's flank. "Good-bye, old feller. You've
been a right good 'un," he said, and strode back to unload
his catch.

"You noted that, I hope," Stormfleet whickered. "Hop
up, and let's be going." The cito trotted Gom along the
boardwalk, and through the early morning streets, scarcely
curbing his impatience. Hungry again, no doubt.

The sun was scarcely up as they climbed the stretch
from the market. They passed under the stable arch into
the yard—and there was Carrick, Shadow at his heels.
At the sight of Gom, the hound began leaping and running around in excited circles.

"Gom!" The master tinker came to meet him, hands outstretched. He clasped Gom by the shoulders and looked him up and down. "Of all the lucky days! Would you know, I've only just got in myself—I've just bedded Finnikin down!" He stroked Stormfleet's neck. "This the horse Essie was telling me about? Come on, let's get him in beside Finnikin, and give him breakfast."

"Brrrgh, a man after my own heart," Stormfleet remarked, as Gom led him after the tinker into the stable, and down to the end stall. There, Shadow started in with sudden loud bark, protesting the intrusion into what he considered his own personal territory.

"Here, sir!" Carrick commanded sternly. "Quiet!" He waved Shadow next door. "Get in with Finnikin. Now lie down, and be still!"

Together, Carrick and Gom gave Stormfleet a bag of oats, and a fresh pail of water. "His coat looks in need of a currycomb, Gom," Carrick said. "You can borrow mine later, if you like."

"Why, thank you, Carrick." Gom lightly rapped Stormfleet's side. "You imposter," he murmured. "If only they could see your real coat!"

"This is my real coat," Stormfleet said. "And it would be glad of a comb from a kindly hand, when you're ready. But not while I'm having my oats."

"Bah," said Gom. "I'll be back." He went with Carrick over into the inn. Essie greeted them hurriedly, ushered them upstairs, where the table was already laid with porridge, and strawberry jam, and oatcakes, and bright yellow butter, and a pot of tea.

"So," Carrick said at last. "Essie tells me you've had some excitement."

Gom eyed his empty plate. Caution warned him to say nothing, yet here was a man who'd risked his own life to save him, who'd spent freely to feed and shelter him, no questions asked, and whose coins still jingled in Gom's pocket. This was a friend no less than Stormfleet, and one he'd readily trust with his secret—if only he were free to speak.

"Nay, don't look so uneasy," Carrick went on. "I had to mention it, or else how could I face Hort and Mudge come next spring when they ask after you? I gave my word I'd look out for you, you know." He smiled as Gom's face fell. "Not that I wouldn't anyway, of my own inclination."

"We—ell," Gom said. "I can tell you some of it."

Carrick nodded gravely. "I wish you would, Master Gom."

"When I left you in the market that day, I met with Zamul."

Carrick leaned back, clasped his hands behind his head. "Go on."

"He—he wanted—something I had. He chased me back to the inn."

"I hope he didn't get it," Carrick said, looking straight at Gom's chest.

Gom's hand went to the old place, closed about the vanished rune. "No, he did not. Anyway," he went on hurriedly, "I hid in a solahinn wagon, and sort of, well, got myself locked in."

Carrick whistled.

Gom told how he'd been forced to dance by the fire, of Jofor's bargain, and how he'd been thrown into the wild horse pen to die. How the cito had let him on its back, how the wild herd had stampeded to freedom. The more Gom spoke, the more preposterous he knew it all must sound.

Carrick cocked his head. "I thought you didn't ride, Master Gom."

"I didn't—don't—didn't." Gom stared intently at his empty teacup.

"And so that is why Urolf's after you," Carrick went on at last. "I must say I can't blame him. He'll hound you from one end of Ulm to the other until he has that cito back. Where is it, by the way?"

Gom kept his head down. "I set it free," he said.

"Ummm." Carrick tipped his chair forward and leaned across the table. "I can believe that, the way you spoiled Shadow. I'm stuck with him now, you know," he added, but didn't sound too displeased. "What happened to Zamul?"

"He—had an accident."

"Accident?"

"Accident," Gom repeated firmly. "He's dead."

"I see." Another whistle. "Master Gom, there's a couple of things still bothering me."

"Oh?"

"After you got taken by the solahinn, how come you met with Urolf *clear across Ulm* only days after?"

"The cito was fast," Gom suggested, hopefully.

"And you don't ride. Umm. Never mind. One last thing."

"Yes?"

"You get back here, Jofor's waiting for you. He grabs you, roughs you up a bit, and Essie rushes to your rescue, no? But one shake of your staff," Carrick went on as Gom didn't respond, "and he takes to his heels, mouthing something about you not being all you seemed."

Gom waited.

With a sudden smile, Carrick reached for Gom's hands and held them fast. "It's all right," he said. "I know there's more to you than meets the eye—as Hort and Mudge did, too, love 'em. But 'tis nothing wrong, we all know that as well. Them, and me, and Essie—we stand by you, against Jofor and Urolf, and Leochtor's whole army, if need be." He let Gom go and stood up. "Time to work. Are you inclined to patching pots?"

Gom scrambled to his feet. After supper in the parlor he'd make his pitch for Riffik. Until then, he had some debts to repay. He dipped his hand in his pocket for Carrick's coins and held them out.

Carrick pushed them aside. "Them's wages on account," he said. "Come on, let's hurry. The morning's half gone and I haven't got my awning up yet!"

On his way through the market, Gom kept out a weather eye for Mat's new pitch, but in vain. Had he been run out, or given up the idea of wizardry for now and gone off on another sort of Bragget jig until the fuss died down? Gom thought not. Perhaps he'd take a turn about the marketplace during his break, and search the far corners. Reaching Carrick's spot, he set down his share of the bundles and helped to set up the tinker's stall.

"There." Carrick stood back to survey the flapping green-and-white striped canvas. "We're ready to set out the gear."

Gom knelt, unstrapped one of the sturdy packs that

contained the tinker's tools. Hammers, clippers, strips of solder neatly coiled, and small, thin iron sheets ready to cut for holes of various sizes. By the time they were ready for business, a large crowd waited with leaky pots and pans. Although, as Carrick himself had said, the market was large enough for twenty tinkers to ply their trade the year around, Carrick was a master, one of the best. Now that he was back, folk who'd waited for his services were clamoring for immediate attention.

They worked steadily all morning, Gom cutting patches, Carrick heating them on a little brazier then shaping them with his hammer to the curve of the pot, and fixing them into place. They were so inundated with work that Gom never got a chance to search for Mat, or even to think of him, much. Near noon, they stopped to eat the elevenses that Essie sent them, then they went on again, through the afternoon heat. As Gom cut away, his mind turned anxiously to the coming evening. After supper, he must sit in the parlor, give Bokar Riffik's pass phrase: the winds of change are blowing. Then what? Wait, he supposed, for whoever to come and tell him where to go, and when.

Gom handed up another patch, restacked waiting pots and kettles. He looked out into the crowded sunshine. Ordinary folk, going about their business, buying clothes and food and knickknacks, gossiping about ordinary daily things. It was hard to believe that not too far away sat the close and secret conclave of the Covenance, maybe down one of those very streets just off the marketplace. Essie had said that the fishing quarter was different from the rest of Pen'langoth, a world within a world. To think of all that magic gathered in one place; all those wizards steeped in mystic lore: wonder was he didn't *feel* the power growing all around him.

The winds of change are blowing . . .

His chest shrank so tight he had to press it with his fist.

The shadows lengthened, the crowds began to thin out, some.

"Another half hour, Master Gom," Carrick said, "and we'll call it a day."

Gom nodded, ready to jump to and pack up, and as he did so, he suddenly remembered Mat. Too late to look now. Maybe tomorrow. He wiped his sleeve across his brow, thinking of the little attic room, a good brisk wash, supper.

All at once, there came an angry shout from over the booth tops, and another, and another, until there was a whole chorus of howling like some pack of ferocious beasts after prey.

Carrick looked up, hammer poised. "Uh-oh. There goes *The Growler*."

"The Growler?"

"That ruckus." The tinker pointed his hammer outside. "Someone's for it—sold a dud, or stolen something. And folk are running him from the market—what's left of him, by the sound of it."

Gom stared outward at the crowds, his ear cocked to the fierce shouts, with a sinking feeling. He'd scarcely reached his feet when a frantic figure erupted into the space before the booth.

"Mat!" Gom's stool went over.

The figure turned, startled. "My dear fellow!"

Shadow sprang up, bristling, teeth bared.

The youth shrank, his glance shifting from Shadow to Gom to Carrick then out into the crowd.

"Quiet!" Carrick commanded Shadow. "Lie down!"

Shadow subsided with a halfhearted bark.

Mat appealed to Carrick. "Hide me, dear sir, will you—please?"

"I don't know," the tinker said, with a frown. "Gom?"

"Please," Gom said quickly. The sounds were getting closer. "He's a friend!"

Carrick stood up, moved aside. "Here—get you down behind my stool."

Mat sprang, folded incredibly fast into the narrow space between seat and canvas. Carrick piled up pots and kettles around the youth, then sitting down again, picked up hammer and pot and began tapping away—just as a pack of angry fishermen pushed through the crowd from various directions, meeting up in front of Carrick's tent.

"He's gone! Vanished!" cried one, scratching his head.

"Can't have," panted another. "I was watching this way all the time."

They turned to the tinker's booth. "Hey up, Carrick," said the first. "You haven't seen 'un running past here, have you?"

"Tall," the second fisher chimed in. "Rod-thin, hair like twine?"

Carrick shrugged. "I see all kinds," he said. "You got trouble?"

"Have we!" A third one folded his arms. "But not as much as what he will when we catch him!"

"Listen," said number one through an angry murmur, "if you spot him, catch a hold and holler, will you?"

The men moved off.

Carrick watched them go, his brows drawn together in a way Gom had never seen before. "I don't know what you did, young fellow," Carrick said quietly, without turning his head, "but whatever, 'twas wrong, and I don't hold with that. So you get you gone and thank your stars that Master Gom's your friend."

Mat popped up in a clatter of falling pans from behind the tinker's seat, stepped gingerly over Shadow. As he brushed past Gom, he threw him a rueful look. "I give up, I really do," he murmured, and took off, with neither please nor thank you.

Gom watched after him sadly.

"Hummm," Carrick said. "Some friend you have there. Where in Ulm did you find him?"

Gom sat down. "He was in Bragget—you know, the one they were going to flog. When he ran, they caught me, and were going to whip me instead—would have but for Shadow. I suppose," Gom said thoughtfully, "if it weren't for Mat, Shadow wouldn't be here!"

Carrick raised his brows. "And I should thank him for that?" He set his hammer down. "Come on, let's pack up. I've a taste in my mouth that needs some rinsing out."

That evening, as Gom went into the parlor to sup with Carrick, he looked covertly around the crowded room, searching each face as before, still saw no one out of the ordinary.

The winds of change are blowing . . .

He gazed around at the bright polished brasses, the glowing wooden floor, the comfortable chintz settles, smelled the warm odors of Essie's good supper. Of those faces crowded around Essie's parlor tables, which was the one? Which of those men—or women—would take the invocation secretly to Bokar Riffik?

Gom was too wrought up to eat: excited, but also a bit afraid. He looked across at Carrick, studied the friendly, weathered face. And at Essie across the room, bent over someone's table. And Brody, running around with loaded trays.

The moment he said those words, he'd commit himself to going off with a total stranger for seven years. Seven years! And when he returned to this place, things wouldn't be the same. Weren't the same already, after talking with Harga. Life in the inn would go around and around in its well-oiled tracks, while his would lead him to a point more distant than his master's house. . . *When you hold the Covenance's scroll of necromancy, then you'll climb this stair, not alamar, but for real . . .*

The room dimmed, and for a moment he was not in Essie's parlor, nor in the misty sky hall, but somewhere far away and in-between. His fork clattered to his plate.

"Hey, lad," Carrick said.

Essie bustled over. "Look at this dish," she scolded. "You haven't eaten, and you're pale as porridge. Do you feel well?" She laid a hand on his forehead. "You're cool enough. Perhaps it's all this excitement, do you think, Carrick?"

"It's been hot, and Gom worked hard. What he needs, Essie, is a jug of your physick. That'll bring his color back."

Gom and Carrick settled themselves by the ingle. Someone struck up a song, and another, and another. As each passing moment brought Gom closer to saying the invocation, his head began to throb with excitement. The air was close, and the noise deafening. Surely no one would hear him over that? Yet Harga had assured him that it was so. As he cleared his throat, Brody brought ale for Carrick, cider for Gom. She set down the mugs, then offered Gom a small bowl piled with sweetmeats.

"Hey up, lad," Carrick said. "Essie's spoiling you tonight."

"Not Essie," Brody blurted, and ran.

"Well." Carrick lifted his mug, saluted Gom. "You've done all right there, Gom. A comely wench, that, never lacking followers."

Yes, Gom thought, watching Brody moving away. And a few days before he'd been quite overcome at the thought. Now? He offered Carrick a sweet, then set the bowl on the table before them. What would Brody be like in seven years? Still serving ale, or married with babies in her lap? And would he care? "The winds of change are blowing," he muttered, and looked up startled. He'd said the invocation, quite without meaning to. He scanned the room, but nobody seemed to be paying him any mind. Should he say it again?

"Essie was right," the tinker said. "You don't look so good, Master Gom. You want to go upstairs?"

Gom thought fast. He'd given the invocation. There was nothing more he could do—except perhaps to go outside and try to clear his throbbing head. Maybe he and Stormfleet could take a turn around the deserted market, in the dark and the quiet. "I think I'll get a bit of fresh air first," he said. He bade Carrick and Essie a good night, then went out to the stables.

* * *

They walked around the market's silent peripheries; along the narrow cobbled thoroughfares that marked the square. From the corner of the inn street, they turned right, going parallel with the lake along the market's southern side. Then they turned left, downhill toward the lake, by the square's eastern border. Onto this road opened many smaller streets, narrow, dark lanes and alleyways overgrown with privet hedge and mulberry, looking closed and mysterious.

"Well, I said it," Gom remarked at last.

"Good." Stormfleet clopped along beside him. "Now what?"

"We wait." Gom stopped at the corner of an alley. "I wouldn't be a bit surprised if the wizards weren't meeting down one of these."

Stormfleet peered over a hedge. "The houses are small. How would they all fit into one of those places?"

"Ah," Gom said. "Perhaps I'll be able to tell you that very soon!"

"When you get your master," Stormfleet said. "What of me?"

"Why, you will come with me, won't you?"

"Since you ask, I think I'll tag along," Stormfleet said, offhandedly.

Gom put his arms about the cito's neck and squeezed hard. "I'm glad."

"Strong words," Stormfleet snorted. "I'll hold you to them!"

They walked on.

At each street corner, wooden posts telling their various names tilted at crazy angles. Gom could see their signs quite plainly in the bright starlight. Bluebell Lane, the first sign said: a sprig of peeling bluebells on a cracked green ground. Next, Skittle Alley, with its fresh-painted sign of three wooden skittles. Pine Street after, then Crocus Street. The fifth sign down sported a man trimming a bright green hedge with gigantic shears. What would that be, Gom wondered. Clipper Street? Shear Alley? He went on. At the lower corner of the market, they turned left again, and walked the wide aisle dividing market from fish mart, between silent, empty stall and slab. A last left turn, and they were climbing uphill along by the western edge, and back to the street where the inn was.

The tour complete, they went around again. Occasionally, the night quiet was broken with boisterous laughter and singing as folk made their way home from the inn. One more round, then Gom walked Stormfleet back to his stall. After, he went to climb the attic stairs at last, passing a still-crowded and noisy parlor, catching a glimpse of Carrick on Essie's settle by the fire, waving his mug and singing with the rest.

Gom was just about to pull off his boots when there came a tap on the door.

He went quite still, not breathing. The summons— already? He crept to the door, stood against it. "Who's there?"

"It's I, Mat. Let me in, I beg you!"

Gom breathed out. Mat? He raised the latch, opened the door a crack, and Mat fell through.

"Forgive me, dear fellow, for bothering you. You don't mind?"

Gom closed the door behind him. "No-o. What's up?"

Mat flopped down in the nearest armchair. "That terrible scene this afternoon! Those crude, boorish men!" He shuddered. "All because they failed to follow my directions!"

"What do you mean?" Gom took the chair opposite.

"They asked me to make them something to help them see better in the dark—for their night fishing, you know? I said no, but they begged and pleaded, so I went to great trouble to devise—" Mat's index finger poked the air. "Very difficult, that's why I had to charge so much. I told them, I *insisted,* 'Take one tablespoon per day, no more.' They can't have listened, for now they claim that while they see no better, they can no longer stand the smell of fish, either!" He rubbed his hands together delicately. "So now they're screaming for their money back, all over town."

"So return it, and have done with them." Seemed simple enough to Gom.

Mat threw up his hands. "If only I could! But it went to keep body and soul together, and a roof over my head. Now even that's lost, for thanks to their vulgar clamor, my landlady's turned me out to starve." He slumped forward in the chair, head in hands.

Gom eyed him in sympathy. Mat had clearly meant to do good. And it was not his fault if his intentions had gone awry. Pity Mat had never had a decent chance in life. And never would, for how could his friend become a wizard without a pass phrase? Unless—he sat up—he gave Mat Folgan's!

No. Gom leaned back again. He'd been sure of Tolasin, and look what happened there. If for some reason Bokar Riffik couldn't or wouldn't take him either, he'd need that phrase himself. Much as he wanted to help Mat, he must wait. When Bokar Riffik was secured, then Gom could pass the phrase on. Meanwhile, he could try to help Mat some other way. "I'm sorry for what happened," Gom said. "Can I do anything?"

Mat's head came up. "Well, perhaps, dear fellow." He flapped a hand weakly. "I haven't eaten for two days and I'm feeling very low."

"Two days!" Gom jumped up. Why, that was terrible! "Wait here, and I'll fetch you something right away."

Mat's eyes flickered. "That's very decent of you." He leaned back and closed his eyes.

At the door, Gom hesitated. His pack lay by the back wall, and Carrick's gear. He tutted impatiently. Mat might be wrong-headed, but he was no thief! Shame on him for even thinking it! Gom closed the door and ran downstairs.

Essie, delighted to think that Gom's appetite had returned, sent him back upstairs with a loaded tray.

Mat lay in the chair, eyes closed, lightly snoring. He started up when Gom tapped him on the shoulder. "Oh, dear fellow! I'm so exhausted, I confess I had fallen deeply asleep!" He took the tray. "This all for me? How can I ever thank you!"

Mat ate hungrily, greedily, and in silence.

"What are you going to do now?" Gom asked, as Mat pushed back the empty tray and stretched out his long legs to the hearth.

"Oh, steal away like a whipped dog," Mat said. "Find some corner to lie in." He laughed nervously.

Gom fumbled in his pockets, took out his new-earned coins, held out the biggest. "Get yourself a bed, and some breakfast. I'll save you some of my elevenses, if you can drop by Carrick's tent tomorrow afternoon."

Mat took the coin with a flourish. "Why, thank you," he said, bowing low. "Thank you, thank you, thank you."

Gom shifted uncomfortably. He hadn't done so very much. But he dared not offer more until he heard from Riffik. He glanced to the door. "I'd let you stay the night here," he said, "but this is not my room."

Mat jumped up, made for the door. "I quite understand. Your tinker friend doesn't exactly like me. Well, not to give offense. I'm only too grateful for the crumb of comfort you could offer me." He glanced to the empty tray. "Well, until tomorrow." He opened the door, then turned, seeming to hesitate. "Tomorrow," he said abruptly, and closed the door behind him.

Gom undressed, and got into bed. He lay awake for some while, his head full of the new master he was to take. . . He awoke suddenly to hear rustling by the back wall. A shadow was bent over, pulling things out of Carrick's bags.

He leapt up. "Hey! Who's there?"

"Sorry, Master Gom." The figure straightened.

"Carrick!" Gom looked at the floor, puzzled. The man's gear was strewn all about, as though he'd been rummaging for something—in vain.

"Have you—?" Carrick began, then broke off, and waved Gom back into bed. "Never mind," he said. "I must have left it out in the stables. Good night."

" 'Night." Gom lay down, thinking, left what out in the stables? Something the man valued very much, it seemed. He slid back down under the covers, the vaguest hint of a worry fretting the edge of his mind.

Chapter Seventeen

THE NEXT MORNING, rain hung in the air. Gom ate his oatcakes absently, then went to see Stormfleet. He fed him, brushed him down, then went with Carrick to the market. Would word come to him in that crowded place? It seemed unlikely, but then The Jolly Fisherman had seemed an unlikely place to give the pass phrase, and Pen'langoth, an unlikely place for the Covenance. *I suppose one never knows with wizards,* he thought. Walking on through the drizzle, he and Carrick merged with the vendors bringing in their wares to sell, passed those already setting out their stalls.

Gom helped unpack pots, then, picking up his cutting tools, he bent to his work. He thought of Mat, hoped his friend had found shelter for the night. When Mat came by at elevenses, Gom would persuade him to keep in close touch somehow, without giving anything away yet about the pass phrase. He pictured giving Mat Folgan's invocation, and Mat's delight: *My dear fellow, thank you, thank you, thank you!* Deep into his own thought, it was a while before Gom noticed Carrick's silence. "Is anything wrong?"

The tinker grunted. "Since you ask," he said. "Some of my gear's gone missing, and I can't think how or where."

Gom's stomach shrank. "Gear?"

"A new, fine-gauge tool kit. Picked it up in Hornholm last week. I swear I took it into the inn with me yesterday, but it's not in any of these packs. Nor in the stable with the rest of my stuff. Here, sir!" The last to Shadow who was sneaking out around the corner of the tent. Tail down, the hound flopped beside Carrick's seat and settled his head on his paws.

"That's what you were looking for last night?"

"Aye," Carrick said. "Essie had a little taffy pot as needed attention. I thought I'd fix it for her before I went to bed."

"Perhaps you left it behind somewhere," Gom suggested hopefully.

Carrick shook his head. "Not that kit." He sighed. "A really good one is hard to come by. That one was the neatest I've yet found for fixing small vessels. Don't know where I'll get another."

"How . . . big was it?"

Carrick put his palms together, so, and so. "About yea big, and light."

Small enough to slip into one's pocket, Gom thought, recalling how he'd left Mat alone in the attic long enough to open Carrick's packs and look them through. He shook off the thought. "Someone could have taken it whilst we were in Essie's parlor," he said. "The attic's never latched, and those back stairs are easy climbing."

Carrick nodded doubtfully.

"Anyone could sneak up when no one was looking," Gom said.

"Anyone could," Carrick agreed. "But for a tinker's gear?"

Gom stared down at the patch he was shaping. The kit could still have been misplaced, he told himself. Or lost, or left somewhere, whatever Carrick said. Except that . . . He recalled Mat the night before, hesitating at the door, as though— Oh! He'd overcut, spoiling the patch. With a *tcha* of annoyance, he set it aside, took up a fresh sheet to start again. Mat had not taken the kit: Gom must not even think of it!

As the morning passed, the rain stopped, and the crowds thickened, bringing a brief rush on Carrick's tent that started Shadow barking excitedly. Repairs piled up until there was scarce room to move. After elevenses— at which Mat didn't show up—a watery sun broke through. Gom cut away, so busy that he forgot about his friend, and even wizards and their pass phrases.

A large shadow fell across the awning. A woman in a flowered apron and galoshes was looking in. "Are you Carrick, the master tinker?"

"Aye, ma'am." Carrick stood up. "What can I do for you?"

" 'Tis my copper kettle for making starch," she explained. "Too big for a widow woman to carry through this crowd. If I could have a hand . . ."

"Certainly." Carrick laid his hammer aside, but she waved him back.

"For shame, to see a fine skilled man like you doing your own donkey work while your apprentice sits idle!"

Carrick smiled. "Gom's not really my apprentice, but kindly helping me, like, ma'am." The tinker turned to Gom. "Gom? Would you mind?"

"Not at all." Gom jumped up and followed the woman

to the street, where a small pony cart waited, and in it, a great, round, copper kettle with a hole in the bottom big as a penny.

"Here you are, lad. Tell Maister Carrick someone will fetch it in four days' time." She reached over, helped Gom lift it out onto the sidewalk. Then she smoothed down her apron, and made to climb up into the cart. And as she did so, she spoke again, her voice now quick and quiet. "Listen well, for this gets said but once: go to the end of Hedgeman's Lane tonight between the hours of twelve and three. Don't bring baggage. Come then, or not at all. Floxie!" She tuttupped loudly to the pony. "Let's go!"

The cart started forward, and rumbled off along the cobbled street. A moment later, the woman, the cart were lost in the traffic.

Gom stood staring after them, the kettle at his feet. The summons! And from such an unexpected source! Come to the end of Hedgeman's Lane, she'd said. He ran his hand through his hair. That must be the street he'd passed the night before, with the sign of the man holding giant shears. He gazed in growing excitement to the market's eastern edge, out of sight now through the crowds. *No baggage.* That spoke of interview. Then would Harga's promise be fulfilled. In just a few hours, he'd have his new master! After that, he'd need his baggage for sure!

He bent, put his arms around the kettle, hoisted it up against his chest. Then, humming faintly, he strode back to Carrick's tent.

The tinker was sound asleep when Gom crept out of bed and slipped on his clothes. Boots in hand, he trod quietly down the stairs, close by the wall, dodging the creaks. At the bottom, he tiptoed through the hall to the back door, which was always left unlocked, and out into the stable yard. There, he sat on the step and pulled on his boots. Across the yard, just inside the stable door, the night watchman sat, oiling tack. He well knew Gom, made no fuss at Gom's going for Stormfleet at that hour.

"Ready?"

"Ready," Stormfleet said. Gom opened the wicket and let him out.

They turned into the street and down, over wet, slippery cobbles, Gom's boots and Stormfleet's hooves sounding loud and hollow in the quiet: *click clack, crick crack.* "We sound like a herd," the cito said.

They moved gingerly down the steep hill, on the market's eastern side, past Bluebell Lane and Skittle Alley, Pine and Crocus Streets. There were no stars tonight, only low, thick cloud. Gom couldn't see the street signs, so he counted the posts, one, two, three, four. At the fifth corner, he halted. Hedgeman's Lane, narrow walkway between derelict cottages and unkempt yards.

Stormfleet sniffed the air and backed off. "Doesn't smell too healthy," he said. "You're sure this is it?"

"Yes." Gom led Stormfleet into the deeper dark of rutted track. Somewhere to the left, a dog's gruff bark came twice, then silence. Gom felt his cautious way along. How far, he wondered, and *what lay at the end?*

The road suddenly bent, like an elbow. Stormfleet whinnied softly. "The air's different."

The cito was right. Gom had the distinct feeling he was crossing some sort of threshold. Apart from the dog, the lane behind him had been quiet—the normal quiet of early hour when folk slept in their beds. But past this corner lay a deeper hush, as though they were in another place. They went on, until, all at once, solid hedge blocked their way: the end of the lane. Gom cast about, found a gap to his left, and a rough brick path. "You stay here, Stormfleet. I'll see what's yonder," he whispered. The path led to a small, two-story stone cottage with shuttered windows and sagging porch. Gom climbed the porch steps and raised his hand to knock. Before his knuckles touched the door, it opened soundlessly, and Gom was pulled into a poky hall, ill-lit.

"Wait." A man's voice, high and shaky with age. The man, small and dry as a bird, left Gom just inside the door, shuffled off into the interior. Before Gom, a flight of bare wooden steps led to the second floor. Past the stair, a ragged crack of light showed under a door.

The man reappeared suddenly, and pointed. "This way."

He led Gom to the door, opened it, and ushered him into a windowless cubbyhole. In it was a small table, two chairs, and an oil lamp turned low.

"Sit." The man waved at the far chair, and went out, closing the door behind him.

Gom squeezed around between wall and table, pulled out the chair, and sat straight, hands clasped on the table before him, eyeing the door eagerly. A board creaked. There came a soft footfall on the stair. Then silence. Presently, Gom slid his hands off the table, placed them on his knees. When would the wizard come?

Gom thought ahead to the interview, to what Bokar Riffik would say, and what he would reply. Name? Gom Gobblechuck. Where from? Windy Mountain. Father?

Stig, woodsman. *Dead, now.* Mother? Would Riffik need to ask?

The door opened, and in walked not Riffik, but the kettle wife, in long gray sash and robe, just like Tolasin's. Not wizard's messenger, Gom saw with surprise, but wizard!

She sat, produced a small round mirror on a brass stand, and set it on the table between them. "I am Potra, Summoner to the Covenance. Look into the glass."

Gom obeyed. His face looked awful at that hour, and in that light: yellow, with purple rings beneath the eyes. The glass flashed, dazzling him. He blinked, looked again to find his image gone, and in its place a hooded graybeard: Bokar Riffik!

"Ah. You're the applicant?" The voice was mild, even friendly.

Encouraged, Gom looked to the woman for direction, but her eyes were closed. He turned back to the mirror. "Yes, sir."

"Name?"

"Gom Gobblechuck. I come from Windy Mountain. My father is—"

"Yes, yes." Bokar Riffik flapped a hand. "You want to work with me."

"Yes, sir."

"Very well. Potra will tell you what to do."

Another flash, and Gom was once more staring at his own face.

Potra jumped up, jabbed the table with her finger. "Be here, same time, three nights hence. Bring your baggage this time—enough for a long stay in a very lonely place." She laughed shortly. "What I said this morning still applies: fail to show, there'll be no second chance."

"Oh, I won't, ma'am," Gom said quickly.

Potra looked skeptical. "I've heard that before! Come." She walked him to the door, where the old man waited, then went upstairs.

"Don't mind her," the man said behind his mottled hand. "She's not so grim as she sounds." He leaned forward confidentially. "Someone got promoted over her this year. She'll recover, in time." He leaned close, squinting up into Gom's face. "Do I know you?"

Gom stepped back. "I've never been here before," he said.

"Oh, well." The old man put his hand to the latch. "When you've seen as many faces as I have . . ." He opened the door, waved Gom through, and walked him down the path. "I'm Junco, the janitor. This place don't look much, do it?" He sniffed. " 'Tisn't their real meeting place, you know. Only where they pick up their new apprentices after the Covenance. Covenance!" He laughed. "That's what they call firing off seven years' pile of grudge and feud over a table shaped like a horseshoe. You know what horses do with them, don't you?" He smacked his backside smartly. "Sitting around that thing with them gray shimmies on, they look like a peck of wood pigeons." He laughed again. "I daresay you're thinking I'm disrespectful. Well, if you'd been around as long as I have, you'd feel free. Why, I was sweeping up when most of them were no higher'n you. This horse yours?"

Gom blinked. It was pitch-dark, and Stormfleet hadn't so much as flicked his tail. "Yes."

"Come, boy." Junco reached up and patted Stormfleet's back. "He feels like a real good crittur. He's your friend."

"Yes," Gom said. They walked on, Stormfleet clopping alongside.

"Lucky," Junco said. "Horse like that's better'n any human. They'll do you down sooner or later, but never one of these."

I don't know, thought Gom. Hort and Mudge had saved his life; Carrick, too. Essie had taken him without a blink. And Mat had given him a penny, which he could ill afford, and had almost promised to find him a wizard. He couldn't imagine any one of them letting him down.

Junco pulled up. "Here we are." They'd reached the elbow in the road. "Go home and get some rest, lad," he said. "Even if you did pick an easy one, Riffik will still take his money's worth!"

"Thank you—and good night," Gom called, but the old man had vanished.

Gom rode Stormfleet back to the inn, saw him into the stable, then undressing quietly, crept into bed. He looked across the room to Carrick's sleeping form. Two hours, they'd be having breakfast and going to the market—as though it were just another day. He stared up at the ceiling. A master at last! It had been all too easy! For once, his plans had not gone astray. Come three nights hence, Potra said. Wouldn't Harga be pleased! Gom drew his knees up. Well, probably, he thought. But with luck, his mother wouldn't ask what happened to Folgan.

Now he must find Mat, give him Folgan's pass phrase. Pity his friend hadn't turned up at the booth. Those men must still be after him. Only three more days to go. Gom sat up. If Mat missed out now, he'd have to wait until Perelion completed his next seven-year round.

Or forever.

Gom nodded resolutely. He must find Mat tomorrow.

Chapter Eighteen

NOON THE NEXT DAY, and still Mat had not come. "Carrick," Gom said, rewrapping the remains of his elevenses. "Would you give me leave for a bit?"

The tinker looked up in surprise. "Good gracious, lad, why should you ask me that? What you do for me is entirely by your own choice."

Gom stepped out from under the shade of the booth, then turned back. "Did you find your kit?"

Carrick shook his head. "I'm beginning to think you spoke true, Master Gom. That somebody did sneak up those stairs and help himself. But who? And why that particular kit and nothing else? It doesn't make sense."

It did, thought Gom, if, on the spur of the moment that kit looked useful and worth something, yet small enough to tuck away in one's pocket. Mat had left the room pretty fast, and without too much persuasion. "Won't be long," he said, and pushed off into the throng. He had no idea where he was going, only that he wanted to let Mat see him—if Mat were about—and a chance to talk to him alone.

As Gom wandered through the crowds, he kept passing the cutler's booth, and his favorite knife. Someone else would buy it now, he thought sadly. He picked it up, weighed it on his palm.

"Hey, young feller. You're wearing it out. Shall I put it by until you've saved your pennies?"

Gom set it down. "Thank you, no."

"Who you with? I haven't seen you but these past few days."

Gom backed off. "Carrick, Carrick the tinker—but I'm leaving," he said. He moved on, and kept moving, for if he stayed by any stall too long, somebody tried to sell him something. He paused by a table piled with shells of all shapes and sizes, picked up a fan of coral delicately shaded pink. He wafted it over his face, thinking of Essie. He held it out to the vendor. "How much?"

"To you—sixpence only."

Sixpence! Gom dipped his hand in his pocket, took out his coins. A moment later, he went on, the coral fan safely wrapped. He looked around. Still no sign of Mat. He should be getting back to Carrick. For shame, leaving the tinker with all the work, for a wild-goose chase!

On his way, he passed a booth hung with curios: cows' horns, faded watercolors on old parchment, parasols full of holes; dried flowers whose origins one could not even guess at, mediocre wooden carvings, bright glass baubles, and dusty paperweights.

A glint of half-buried silver caught Gom's eye. He stopped. Another death's-head? Gom nudged the clutter aside, and drew out an ancient metal kerchief ring. He breathed out: no sign of skull. Silly, he thought. Why should there be? He held it to the light, caught his breath again, but in delight. A serpent, like Ganash, but more sinuous and slender, coiled on itself three times, then took its own tail into its mouth. A wondrous design, and well wrought. Gom held the ring against his neck.

It would be nice to have a reminder of the kundalara. But, he took it away again. He didn't wear kerchiefs, and didn't he have enough to worry about with silver ring and crystal in his pouch? Now Carrick—he had but a plain copper kerchief ring, which he wore every day. Gom turned to the booth-keeper. "How much?"

"For you, young man—five shillings only!"

Gom's face fell. Five shillings! He had only eighteen pence remaining in his pocket. Crestfallen, he set the ring down and turned away.

"Hey—don't you want to bargain? How much you got?"

Gom hesitated. He didn't want to leave himself penniless entirely. "I offer one shilling; that's all I can afford."

The man took up the ring, and held out his open palm. "Deal!"

Ring and shilling changed hands, and Gom slipped his prize in his pocket. He instantly felt lighter, happier. He was leaving his friends, but now also leaving something with them!

Gom had almost reached Carrick's tent when Mat popped up in front of him, swathed in faded cloak of purple velvet, and floppy crimson cap. "Dear fellow," Mat murmured, "did you say something about food?"

They went into the shelter of a vegetable stall, ducked down behind the leafy greens. Gom fished in his back pocket, took out the battered remains of his elevenses.

He watched Mat tear open the wrappings, stuff a large piece of bread and cheese into his mouth. There was a bad feeling inside him, and it wouldn't go away until he'd spoken out. But how? *When I left you alone in Carrick's attic, did you rifle his belongings and take his fine-gauge tool kit?* He just couldn't. But he had to say something. He must, to clear the air.

"My friend Carrick has lost a tool kit. It was taken from his pack the other night. The night you visited me."

Mat slowly turned his head. "Are you—are you suggesting that I—that I—" He rolled his eyes skyward. "Not you too."

"Did you take it, yes or no?"

"My dear, dear, fellow."

"Yes, or no."

"No." Mat stood up. "I see you don't believe me. I'd best be going." He pocketed the remains of the bread and cheese. Gom caught his sleeve and pulled him down again.

"I believe you," he said. Mat did indeed look most distressed. And, besides, if he'd stolen the kit, he'd not be grubbing for leftovers, surely.

Mat consented to let himself be drawn. "I think some kind of apology is in order," he said.

Gom nodded. Fair enough. "Sorry. Listen, you must come to Essie's parlor for just a minute tonight."

Mat looked guarded. "Why?"

"Do you recall telling me you had ambitions?"

"Indeed!"

"What if I said I could get you apprenticed this very Covenance?"

"You mean—" Mat's eyes narrowed. "What do you know about that?"

"A little—enough to help us both." Gom explained about the invocations, how he had one to spare, watching all the while for Mat's delighted shout.

But Mat only frowned. "How did you come by two of these—invocations, when I, who have searched long and far, have found not one?" No *dear fellow*, no *thank you, thank you, thank you.*

"Does that matter? Do you want it, or no?" Come to think, Mat had probably not even heard of the pass phrases, or he'd surely have mentioned them. He should be glad!

"You took the better wizard, I suppose," Mat said.

Gom gaped at him. Why, the ingratitude!

"Oh, well," Mat sighed, "beggars can't be choosers. Sorry, dear chap," he said hurriedly, as Gom stood up. He caught Gom's arm, drew him back down. "I'm not myself today. Do tell me more."

Gom ate supper nervously. Every two minutes or so, he looked to the door, but saw no sign of Mat. Then, just after supper was cleared, and he was moving to Essie's settle with Carrick, the tinker nudged him in the ribs.

"Hey up, lad, there's somebody over by the door looking straight at you. Do you know, he looks familiar, though I can't quite—"

Gom turned his head, saw Mat in cloak and cap, trying to catch his eye. He jumped up, went to the door.

"Dear chap, I can't do it. You see those large men over there?" Mat pointed to a table by the back wall.

Gom nodded. "They the ones who chased you?"

"Oh, at least. Could you—would you do this thing for me?"

"I explained," Gom said. "You have to give your own pass phrase. If you don't, how will whoever know who you are? Besides, I've given mine. If I speak for you as well, they'll think I'm just being greedy!"

"Excuse me, Gom dear." Essie squeezed by, shot Mat a curious look.

"You see?" Mat pulled his hat farther over his face. "Your landlady knew me! They'll all know me! I can't go through with this!"

"Tell you what." Gom jogged Mat's elbow. "Say the words here, by the door, then run!"

Mat's eyes raked the busy room. "You think?" He cleared his throat, turning one or two heads. "I say," Mat declared loudly. "It's awfully hot for the time of year, is it not? They say that even *the crow flies north!*"

All eyes turned to the door.

"Hey up!" One of the fisherman leapt to his feet. "There's that bogus pothykeery!" The fisher's companions sprang up, tipping the table, spilling their ale.

Mat turned and ran, the men pushed past Gom, nearly knocking him over.

"Here," Essie cried sharply. "Wait up!" Reaching the parlor door, she pulled Gom aside. "There's another ruckus starting. Go to Carrick, there's a lamb," she said, and rushed out into the hall after the angry men.

Gom went, at the same time looking around the room, trying once more to spot the wizards' agent, but without success. He leaned back against the settle and took up his cider in satisfaction. The men would give Mat a chase, and Essie would fuss for the rest of the evening. No matter. Mat had given Folgan's invocation. The rest would follow. With luck, Mat was on his way.

The next day, Gom saw no sign of his friend. That evening, he almost slipped out to Hedgeman's Lane to see if Mat had been summoned, but thought the better of it. It was not his business any longer. He'd done his bit. The rest was up to Mat. Besides, other problems weighed on Gom's mind now. Tomorrow night he was leaving, and he'd not yet told Carrick or Essie.

As he and the tinker washed for supper, Gom finally broke the news. "I can't say much, Carrick, but I am apprenticed someplace away from here."

"Well, I'll be—" Carrick sat, slowly mopping his face. "So that was what was weighing on your mind." He set down the towel. "Who's taking you? As what?"

"I—can't say."

The tinker smiled briefly. "All right." He wagged a finger at Gom. "I just might be able to guess something near the truth. Something secret, something—special, not open to ordinary folks. Conjuror—no! Apothecary? You asked me about that up north, as I recall. No. Not that. I see you learning the herb lore, yes, but not making a fat profit from other folks's maladies. Which leaves—necromancer—that it?" Carrick's eyes gleamed. "Oh, yes . . ." he breathed. "I could see you going off to do that. Why—"

Gom looked awkwardly. Trust Carrick!

"I see I'm overstepping myself, Master Gom." Carrick was serious at once. "My apologies, and your secret's safe with me, as you know. You'll be gone awhile."

"Yes." In the silence, Gom heard Carrick's long-drawn breath, in, and out. Neither of them moved.

Then the tinker jumped up. "Come on," he said, in his normal voice. "Let's eat. You're going to tell Essie?"

"Of course!" Gom bit his lip. "But I'm not sure how."

Carrick laughed. "Scared eh, lad? So would I be. Tell you what: I'll have a word with her, after you've gone to bed. Yes, I think that would be better all around. So come on down, eat and drink, there's no knowing when you'll get another chance to be ruined rotten by two doting females!"

It was a long evening, somewhat overmerry and loud. But finally Gom took himself off, and made himself ready for bed. Before he climbed in, he went to the window. The Wanderer had broken away slightly, forming now a close bright triad with Frydd and Munyr.

He turned from the casement, climbed into bed, and lay, unable to sleep. He stared into the dark, thinking of Harga, remembering their second evening out by the orchard when she'd told him of the three, and how she and he had kept Stormfleet company under their light. He heard Carrick come in, get into bed, heard the tinker's breathing deepen, heard a light snore.

On an impulse, Gom got up, threw his coat over his shoulders, and crept down the back stair to the stable.

The cito flicked his tail in sleepy greeting.

Without a word, Gom lay down in the straw, curled up, and slept.

The next day promised to be bright and hot. Carrick urged Gom to go out to enjoy his last hours of freedom, as he put it, but Gom went to the tinker's tent and worked on through the heat. Once, he glimpsed Potra, in her flowered smock. Once, he thought he saw Junco, laden with a large heavy shopping basket, and almost ran to see, but thought the better of it.

Elevenses came and went. Gom saved some bread and cheese, but Mat didn't appear. As the sun went down, Gom toured the market a last time, savoring the crowds, the bright displays. He stopped to look at shirts, aware of his own worn and faded tunic, thinking how shabby he would look to his new master. Sighing, he swung by the cutler's stall for one last look at his knife. It was gone. He closed his empty palm, as though on its handle. It had fitted his hand so perfectly. He could have carved good things with that blade. Gom turned sadly away, hoping that whoever had bought it would use it well.

He helped Carrick pack up the gear and carry it back to The Jolly Fisherman, noticing that the heavy backlog of leaky pots was gone.

"Couldn't have done without you, lad," Carrick said, as they walked up the hill. "If you change your mind, you've a job here, anytime!"

When they arrived at the inn, Essie sent them to wash and make themselves grand, for, she said, they were to have a party in her private parlor. She looked hard at Gom, said nothing, although he could see that she was itching to. What, he wondered, could Carrick have said to make her hold her tongue?

The tiny parlor was stuffed with furniture and curios. There were brass and crystal candelabra shining from roof beam and wall. Everything was smothered in lace: chairs, shelves, the mantel; little carts that held china figurines, and other curios that customers had given her over the years.

The room was warm and close, smelling of Essie's face powder. The hob, freshly black-leaded, reflected the flames of a handsome fire on which a copper kettle sang.

And the table! Essie had thrown a bobbled lace cover over a deep plum tablecloth, and on it set her best silver, and a china tea service painted with pink roses. The cups were so fine and so thin that Gom could see the light through them, while—and Gom had never seen the like, certainly not on any market stall—their rims and handles were trimmed with pure gold!

Essie seated them at the table, and poured tea.

"Well," Carrick said. "I declare I've never seen such a wonderful spread. Essie's done us proud, eh, Gom?"

Gom nodded, overcome, thinking he'd not be able to eat a bite. But when Essie brought out the four-tiered dish of little cakes, and bowls of sweetmeats sprinkled with colored sugar and little silver balls, and sweet biscuits, and trifle, it all found its way down into Gom's middle without too much trouble. And all the while, Essie and Carrick traded tales and anecdotes about their years in the inn that set Gom laughing and forgetting the moment of parting that was to come.

But at last, Essie cleared the table, set out three cups of warm red wine and wished Gom well. Then, going to a chest behind the door, she raised the lace cover, lifted the lid, and took out a soft, flat package.

"Here, Gom. So's you go off looking halfway decent."

Gom took it, wondering, and pulled off the wrapping. Inside were blue breeches of sturdy cotton, and tunic to match.

"Funny," Essie said, as he shook the tunic out and held it against him. "Soon as I saw them, I said to myself, I said, that's him!"

Gom stood up, held the top against him. A perfect fit, and just like the one he'd so admired the day he'd fled Zamul in the marketplace. He put his arms about Essie, hugged her tight. "Essie—thank you."

"On with them, and let's have a look at you," she said, giving him a little shove.

"Wait," Carrick said. The tinker fished in a back pocket, pulled out something wrapped in a kerchief. "Here, Master Gom."

Gom took it, weighed it in his hand. It felt very like— Quickly, he unrolled the cloth. His knife! "Carrick, how did you know?"

Carrick grinned. "Tinkers learn a lot if they use their ears and eyes. Haven't I told you before?"

Gom went around the table, hugged him too. "Thank you, thank you both!"

Carrick nodded, pleased. "Now, go and try them all on, quick. Don't keep us in suspense."

"I'll be but a moment," Gom cried. He ran upstairs, changed into his new clothes. They fit perfectly, felt clean and crisp and comfortable. He put Harga's belt back on, fastened the knife at its side. He stood before the casement, admiring his reflection. He certainly wouldn't look like any old ragamuffin now, he thought. He must be one of the luckiest fellows in the world!

And now it was Gom's turn for surprises. He took out the coral fan and the metal kerchief ring, and ran back downstairs.

"Doesn't he look fine!" Essie cried, as Gom set the gifts down, the coral fan by Essie, the ring on Carrick's place.

Essie took up the coral fan, turned it over. "Well," she said, fanning her cheeks rapidly. "What a rare fine thing! I thank you, Gom dear."

Carrick took up the ancient ring, and held it to the light. "That's fine-wrought. And I do believe—" He held it closer, then rubbed the silver coils with his thumb. "It's a kundalara—one of them sea serpents like in the legends." Carrick closed his hand about it. "I'll bet it could tell a tale or two." He looked up. "It's said to be lucky, you know; to bring prosperity to them as bears its likeness. Thank you, lad. I'll wear it every day."

They sat awhile longer, talking, while the minutes moved on. Then all too soon, it was time for Gom to go.

"You want us to come and see you off, Gom?" Essie's face wobbled.

Gom hesitated. Another leave-taking. "I'd much rather you stayed here." He embraced them, exchanged last farewells, then ran upstairs for his two packs, the old one that Mudge had given him, and Harga's small one. A handful, but they were light, and almost empty save for his spare clothes, and water bottle, since, as he'd told Essie, he'd not be needing much else. He shouldn't, going off with a magical man. He rolled up Harga's pack, and stuffed it into the larger, and to that tied his bedroll. Almost there. He smoothed down his new breeches, tucked in his new shirt, adjusted Harga's belt, then put on his jacket.

Now. Gom gazed around the room, then went for a last look through the casement. Perelion was just clear, and moving out. He took his staff, hoisted his pack, and went down the attic stairs.

Chapter Nineteen

GOM WENT to Stormfleet's stall. "Time to go. Ready?"

Stormfleet pushed the wicket with his nose. "More than. Let's be off."

Gom ducked into Finnikin's stall. "Good-bye for now," he said, patting the horse's sturdy flank. Shadow jumped up, licked Gom's face. "Take care. Trouble seems to have a way of finding you."

"I will," Gom said, scratching the dog's head. "I'll always remember how you saved my hide in Bragget."

"And I, that you found me a wonderful new master. Good-bye!"

Gom and Stormfleet walked briskly down the hill and around the corner, then on; past the signposts one by one, turning down Hedgeman's Lane. They'd not gone far when a hooded shadow brushed by, with a smaller shape—heavily laden—in tow. A wizard, his apprentice tagging after, bent under his new master's gear. Two more pairs passed, one wizard on horseback, the apprentice walking behind. Gom went faster. Bokar Riffik might be waiting for him.

They were just rounding the elbow, when Stormfleet whickered warning, and a tall figure shot out of the dark, and grabbed Gom's arm.

"My dear fellow!" It was Mat, cloaked, hatted, and

out of breath. "Thank goodness I caught you in time! Don't worry," he said, as Gom looked past him. "Our masters haven't yet arrived."

"Folgan took you then," Gom said. "That's good."

"Yes, well." Mat hung his head. "I have such a terrible confession to make. What you asked me the other day —forgive me, I couldn't tell the truth. But now I have this chance to begin my life anew, I want to put things right."

"Carrick's kit?"

"What can I say?" Mat held out his hand. Gom could just make out a long flat box with silver clasps. "Return it for me, please? Say I'm sorry."

"Return it? *Me?*"

"It won't take you a minute."

"But that's for you to do, Mat."

Mat hung his head. "I'm a coward, dear boy, I'm ashamed to admit it." He sighed. "Pity. I'll just have to leave it here, beside the road, for nothing will take me back to that confounded inn!"

Gom eyed the little box, pictured the tools lying in the rain, rusting. Or someone coming by, picking them up, pocketing them. He couldn't stand it. "Here!" He thrust out his hand.

Mat slapped the kit onto Gom's outstretched palm. "My dear fellow—my *friend!*"

"You're sure Riffik hasn't come yet?"

Mat spread his hands. "Would I be here?" He caught Gom's sleeve. "Look," he said. "Help me to make this fresh start. You can do it in plenty of time on your friend there."

Gom slung his staff. "Let's go, Withershins." He

scrambled up, and Stormfleet, wheeling about, trotted back up the lane, then galloped uphill alongside the market, Gom clinging on grimly with his hands and knees, his old hurts starting up again. Under his jacket, his tunic grew warm and damp, giving off a scent of new-dressed cloth.

Stormfleet crossed the street, turned up toward the swinging inn sign. Gom, his middle churning with anxiety, pictured Riffik standing in the hall, looking around for the new apprentice, Junco calling out his name. Gom ground his teeth. Drat Mat, for such a nuisance! And yet he should be glad that his friend was making good at last.

Gom left Stormfleet out in the street, sprinted through the stable yard, tiptoed through the deserted front hall, up the back stairs. He slipped into the attic, crept over to Carrick's bed.

The tinker was lying on his back. On the table at his side lay the Ganash ring, Carrick's best red kerchief folded beside it, ready for morning. Gom reached out, carefully placed the kit box beside it.

Carrick's eyes opened. "Master Gom? Everything all right? You sound puffed."

"Everything's just fine. I'm sorry to wake you. I—found your kit."

The tinker turned his head. "Oh? Where?"

"In the street," Gom said. "Will that do?"

Carrick nodded understanding. "Thank you. Go for your life—and good luck."

Gom bowed awkwardly. He hated good-byes. And second good-byes even more. "Until next time," he said, and fled.

* * *

They galloped headlong down the lane, turned the elbow, dodging three more pairs of figures on the way, no sign of Mat. At the hedge, Gom slid down, ducked through and along the path, knocked on the door.

Junco's ancient face creased in surprise. "What are you doing here?"

Gom eyed him blankly. "What do you mean?"

Junco pulled him inside, shut the door. The tiny hall was crammed with youths standing, sitting about, watching the stairs expectantly.

"That pal of yours—he said you'd changed your mind. Caused a bit of a stink with Riffik standing there, waiting, it did, I'll tell you."

Gom stared in disbelief. "Where's Maister Riffik? I can explain."

"I doubt it," Junco said. "He's gone."

"*Gone?*"

"Aye, ten minutes since. With your friend."

"I don't understand." *Gone? With Mat?*

"Come on." Junco drew Gom past the stair, into the little cubbyhole, and shut the door. "Now sit down." The janitor pulled out the nearer chair and pushed Gom onto it.

Gom's mind was whirling. Mat—gone off with Bokar Riffik! *You took the better wizard, I suppose . . .* Rage started up somewhere inside. The business with Carrick's kit had been a ruse to get Gom out of the way! But Mat could not have known of Riffik. Gom had never said his name. "How?"

Junco leaned on the table. "Well, first time he came

in, I said, Folgan's not here yet. He don't come till last usually, I told him. You got a wait. Just then Riffik comes down the stairs bleating 'Where's that Gom Gobblechuck?' 'He'll be right along, I'm sure, Maister Riffik,' I says. 'I'll let you know the minute he arrives.' That Mat, he looks Riffik up and down, then turns to me. 'Forgot something,' he says. 'Be right back.' Sure enough, he's back inside two minutes. Says he bumped into you in the lane and that you'd changed your mind. Well, I go to tell Riffik, and he comes down the stairs oh dearing and flapping his hands. In the middle of it all, this Mat ups and offers to go with him instead! Highly irregular, Riffik sniffs, but do you know, in two blinks of an eye they're gone. So that's that for you, lad. I mean, you can't complain, for you'd look a fool, and they don't take fools, you see?"

Gom sat dumb. Of all the lies Mat could tell, he'd picked the one to do the most damage! . . . *fail to show, there'll be no second chance.*

"Told you to stick to horses," Junco said. "Didn't I?"

"I have to have a master, Junco," Gom said fiercely. "I shan't leave here without one."

The old man's eyes widened. "I know you now. That look! I'd recognize it anywhere. You're to do with Harga!"

Gom's chin came up. "I'm her son."

Junco clapped his gnarled old hands delightedly. "Well, I never! Son!" He peered at Gom doubtfully. "She know you're here?"

"Yes," Gom said. "And she expects me to leave with a master this night."

Junco shook his locks. "She does? Oh dear. If I could

help you, I would. But everybody's spoken for." He turned at a sudden commotion in the hall. "Wait here. I'm sadly neglecting my door duty." The old man went out.

Gom sat back, still dumbfounded. How could Mat have done such a thing! Why, if Gom ever saw him again . . . no. It was his own fault. Hadn't everybody warned him? He deserved to have been tricked! Fine wizard he'd make, gullible fool that he was!

And now he'd lost his master. Once again, sure plan had gone awry. And yet—what about Harga's spell? He stared down at the table, trying to remember her words. *. . . the magic that I have laid about you should pull a mentor to you . . .* He moved his head slowly from side to side. "Should" was not "will." When he'd asked to have a mentor definitely that year, she'd refused his wish, said he was asking too much. Choose something more modest, she'd told him. Something that you yourself can help along. Well, he had chosen, and she had granted his wish, and now he'd botched it.

He thought bleakly of the crystal stair. It had come to mean so much through the days. His path of commitment, his Onder's bridge. From the time he'd left the Dunderfosse, he'd been climbing it, so he'd thought, but now he saw he'd not even set foot to it yet.

This year, from this very Covenance, he was to have gone off on his seven-year journey. His eyes smarted with bitter tears. What had he done! What long-term peril would his folly bring upon them all? They'd counted on him. You'll do it, I trust you, Harga had said. . . *When you hold the Covenance's scroll of necromancy, then you'll climb this stair . . . for real. Then you'll learn at last the trust that Jastra would vest in you . . .*

He thrust his elbows on the table, buried his head in his hands. No journey now. No crystal stair. Tolasin had called him too anxious. A little more anxiety would not have gone amiss. What else had the wizard said? *You have a knack of bending things your way, in the end.* Gom grunted in self-disgust. Some knack. He'd let Harga down. And Jastra. All Ulm! And he couldn't blame Urolf, or Leochtor, or Tolasin. Only himself. What could he do? The Covenance was truly over. All the other wizards were spoken for.

Gom's head came up slowly. All . . . save one.

Junco came back in. "Two more gone. It's thinning out. Another hour, and I'll finally get some sleep. Sorry lad, that doesn't help you at all." He stood aside to let Gom pass.

"There is another wizard," Gom said, making no move to get up. "The one that should have had Mat."

"*Folgan?*" Junco's mouth fell open. "You speak of Folgan, you, Harga's son?" He shook his head. "As if he'll not be mad enough when he finds Riffik's made off with his boy. But to find you here on top of that —" Junco let out a wheezy whistle. "There's no telling what he may do, and not just to you." He tapped his own chest.

"I'll risk it," Gom said quickly. "Would you get him to see me?"

"You're asking quite a bit," Junco said, shaking his head. "I don't know." He opened the door a slit, and peeked through. "He's just coming," the old man said. "Wait here." He went out, and closed the door behind him.

Gom sat quite still.

A murmur of voices, one rising, a harsh voice, angry.

"What do you mean, gone! He what? Well, what am I going to do now!"

The old man's voice, low, indistinct, then Folgan's in reply.

"Still here? Late? *Late,* you say? What kind of boy is late! You know I don't tolerate such—" Gom couldn't hear the rest.

The door opened. Junco put his head inside and winked. "His nibs is coming to look you over. I didn't say your name."

Gom stood up, bracing himself.

A moment later, the door was flung back and a hooded, bearded figure stood in the doorway. "Junco tells me you came late."

"No, sir," Gom said. "Not exactly, that is—" Junco was waving warning past Folgan's shoulder.

"Well, were you or weren't you?"

It hurt to say it. "Yes." Not only late, but too late to catch Mat.

Folgan was looking at him strangely. "Your face is familiar. Name?"

Gom's mouth was dry. "Gom Gobblechuck, of Windy Mountain."

The wizard eyed him narrowly. "Father?"

"Stig, woodcutter, sir."

"Mother?"

Gom tried to swallow. "Harga, sir. Harga the Brown."

"Harga the Brown!" Folgan raised his staff to Junco. "You half-wit! You'll pay for wasting my time. Throw him out!"

"Wait!" Gom cried. "Do that, and we both lose."

Folgan's brows went up. "How is that?"

"You need an apprentice. I need a master. And here we are."

The brows came down again. "You take me for a fool, boy? I'll not harbor a spy."

Spy! First Urolf, claiming Harga had stolen his precious cito, now this cantankerous old man claiming his mother was after his secrets—and all without a shred of proof! "Not true!" Gom protested angrily. "My mother wouldn't stoop to such a low trick. She told me about you—and she said better things of you than you of her! She said even though you didn't like her, you were fair, and would judge me on my own merits!"

The wizard looked surprised. "She did?"

Gom nodded. "Yes—sir."

"Hummmm." The wizard appeared to consider. "Harga is too clever for her own boots, but she's straight, I'll admit." He pulled on his beard. Then shot Gom a sudden look from under his brow. "How come she's not taking you herself? Well?" he demanded, as Gom stayed silent.

"She said you wouldn't ask that, sir. That wizards didn't ask questions about other wizards."

"Why you young—" Folgan began, then suddenly to Gom's surprise, he laughed. As abruptly, the laughter cut, and Folgan's brows came together. "You'd be quick, I suppose. Less of a fool than most. You realize I'll test you hard, make you work your way."

"Yes." Gom held his breath, crossed his fingers for luck.

Behind Folgan, the door opened and closed. In the silence, Junco smacked his hands together. "The last one," Gom heard him say.

There was only Folgan left. And Gom.

"Yes, well." Folgan picked up a heavy pack from the floor and dumped it with a thud on the table. "Here," he said. "Let's be going."

Gom let go his breath. "Thank you, sir." He slung his staff, his pack, hoisted Folgan's with both hands, and carried it out into the hall. He wanted to whoop, to neigh loud victory through the hedge to Stormfleet, but dared not flaunt his luck. He kept his head down, and his mouth shut.

Junco held the door open. "Good luck, young feller," he murmured behind his hand as Gom passed. "Look out for yourself!"

Folgan was waiting impatiently below. "Where's Hevron, Junco! Come! I haven't all night!" Junco hurried off the porch, vanished around the side of the house.

Folgan leaned on his staff. "You have a horse, boy?"

A horse? Gom set down Folgan's pack. It was very heavy, and of awkward bulk.

"If not," Folgan went on, without a breath's pause, "you'll have to walk behind, and that will slow things up, confound it."

Junco came into sight, leading a sturdy chestnut roan by the halter.

"It seems," Folgan snapped, "that I must ask my questions twice. Have you or have you not got a horse?" Junco held the stirrup while Folgan, hoisting his long gray robe, set his foot and swung himself up in the saddle.

There came a loud whinny from behind the hedge, and a dark gray head poked through the bushes. "Well? Are we going, or aren't we? I've been standing out here for hours!"

Gom looked up at Folgan, his eyes shining. "Oh, I

have a horse, sir. I have indeed! A very fine beast! Come, Withershins. Hup! Hup!"

Stormfleet limped out from cover. Folgan exclaimed. Junco clapped his hands together. Gom lightly swung up onto the bare, bent back.

" 'Withershins, hup!' indeed!" Stormfleet whinnied in disgust. "That your master? He looks mean as an adder! Let's move before he bites!"

Moments later, Gom was riding along behind Folgan up the narrow lane. On either side, bushes whispered in the night dark. Overhead, the Wanderer moved out into the wide darkness of empty space to begin another solitary seven-year journey.

Stig's Song
of the Hearth

Walk-ing home at twi-light, through the mist-y mount-ain
Climb-ing home at twi-light, up a wind-ing mount-ain

air, High a- bove a dark-ling world, with-out a soul to care;
path, To the sound of laugh-ter, and the warmth of op - en hearth,

See a light shine from my door, a sha-dow wait-ing there:
Lov-ing arms emb-race me, child-ren ga-ther round my chair:

Wife, who came in my-ster - y, my lone-ly life to share!
Wife, you came in my-ster - y, a joy-ous life to share.

(guitar chord segment to be played between verses)

The Melancholy Ballad of Hershel the Young Fisherman and His Love Poll

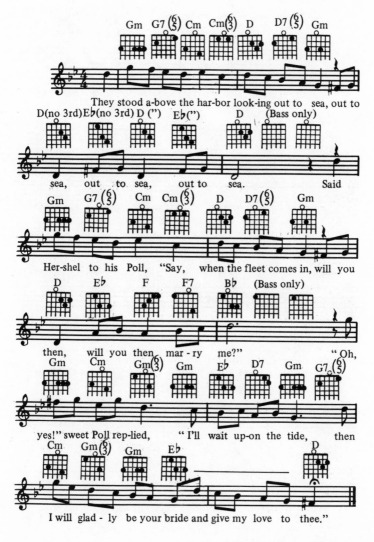

They stood a-bove the har-bor look-ing out to sea, out to sea, out to sea, out to sea. Said Her-shel to his Poll, "Say, when the fleet comes in, will you then, will you then mar-ry me?" "Oh, yes!" sweet Poll rep-lied, "I'll wait up-on the tide, then I will glad-ly be your bride and give my love to thee."

See pages 134-136 for the rest of the lyrics.

Shanty

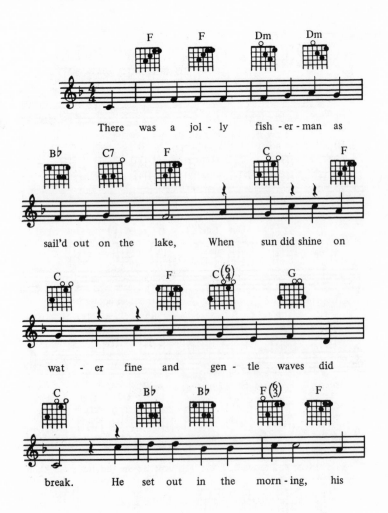

There was a jol - ly fish - er - man as

sail'd out on the lake, When sun did shine on

wat - er fine and gen - tle waves did

break. He set out in the morn - ing, his

wood-en deck up - on; He caught a hake, And a
gard - en rake, And was home by half - past one.

CHORUS:
Then what did our jol - ly man do, (As
true as I tell this tale)? With a ji-ig and a grin, He hove
to by Es-sie's inn—And he call'd for a jug of ale!

See pages 131-133 for the rest of the lyrics.

Gom's Waly

If I could but know where Har-ga has gone,

and the day of her ret - urn - ing;

If I could but learn she mis - ses her son,

and her heart is touch'd with yearn - ing:

But I on-ly know for now   I must go   on,

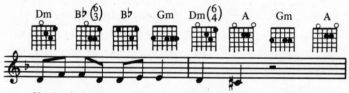

Up the dark, un-cert-ain steps   blind - ly;

Walk the high and nar - row stair,   till I have   done,

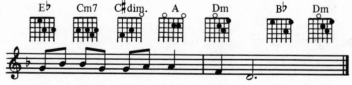

Leave my world fam-il - iar be - hind   me.

Grace Chetwin

has been thinking about Gom Gobblechuck and his history for a long time. After graduating from Southampton University in England, she moved to New Zealand where she married Paddy Roberts. During the busy time after their daughters were born, she taught school and also formed her own dance company. Later her family settled on Long Island, New York, the setting for her first two suspense fantasies, *On All Hallows' Eve* and *Out of the Dark World*. Through it all, she continued to be fascinated with thoughts of what had happened to Gom in the land of Ulm. Then she began to write the TALES OF GOM. The first, *Gom on Windy Mountain*, is the prequel to a trilogy that will include *The Riddle and the Rune*, *The Crystal Stair*, and *The Starstone*.